When the girls arrived at the far corner of the square, they found that the boys had stopped in their tracks!

"Hey, they did wait for us," Rachel said.

But it turned out the boys weren't being polite. They were frozen in place while someone — or something — made its way toward them.

The creature was wrapped from head to toe in gauze bandages. One arm oozed green blood and dangled down by the monster's knees. Its head was a mass of bandages and black spiderwebs (complete with spiders). Its lips were black and shiny, and its teeth — seen through a ghastly smile — were green, yellow, and brown.

The monster was so terrifying, it had to be real!

ROTTEN APPLE BOOKS

Drop-Dead Gorgeous

by Elizabeth Lenhard

ROTTEN APPLE

SCHOLASTIC INC.

For my nieces Rachel and Lindsey, sweet, stylish
wits who provided inspiration for these characters
(except for the zombie parts).

ISBN 978-0-545-58951-2

12 11 10 9 8 7 6 5 4 3 2 1   14 15 16 17 18/0

Printed in the U.S.A.   40
First printing, September 2014

Chapter One

"Nooo," Rachel Harkness cried. "This can't be happening!"

Her legs went wobbly. She began to drop to her knees. Only in the last moment before she hit the pavement did she manage to grab the open door of her mother's car and stop herself.

But she *couldn't* stop her hands from trembling and her heart from racing. She couldn't help but feel a mixture of horror and dread.

"Life as I knew it is over," she whispered. "Completely over."

Her mother put the car in park and leaned into the passenger seat to peer up at her daughter. "Honey, aren't you being a little melodramatic?" she asked. "And aren't you going to be late?"

She gazed past Rachel at the other kids streaming into Slayton Middle School. Unlike Rachel, they all seemed to be wearing jeans and T-shirts and easy smiles.

Instead of hurrying after her classmates, Rachel flopped back into the car. She stared at her mother.

"Who cares about being late?" she sputtered. She pointed at the car radio. "You *did* hear the same thing I just heard on the morning news, didn't you? *The mall is closing*, Mom. Even if it was an entire hour away, even if it didn't have an H&M or an Anthropologie, even if it was probably the worst mall in Iowa, maybe even the whole country, this is a tragedy."

"Rachel," her mother said. "I'm on my way to see a patient with advanced diabetes. *That* is a tragedy."

Rachel sighed. She hated it when her mom played her I'm-a-doctor card to give her perspective. She especially hated when her mom was right.

But even if the mall closing wasn't life-threatening, it was still a big deal to Rachel. Clothes had been her passion ever since preschool, when she'd first learned to mix stripes, polka dots, and really big hair accessories. She had her future all mapped out —

first she'd move to New York, then she'd become a fashion designer, preferably a famous one.

But how can I become a designer if I can't go to stores in person to study fabric and construction? she wondered. *I need to try on shoes and jewelry to style outfits. I need to talk to store managers about trends.*

Rachel knew she couldn't voice these complaints out loud. Her mom was already annoyed that Rachel had missed the school bus while searching for her favorite yellow ballet flats. She clearly had even less patience for the day's second fashion emergency.

So Rachel just said glumly, "Thanks for the ride. Sorry I made you late."

Her mom grimaced with sympathy and ran a hand over Rachel's long, dark-blond hair, being careful not to dislodge any of her purple clip-in hair extensions.

"Listen," her mom said, "I know how important fashion is to you. But you can still get ideas from your magazines and the Internet. And your sewing skills have come so far, you can make anything you want to wear."

"Thanks for trying to cheer me up." Rachel sighed as she opened the car door. "But magazines and the

Internet are *so* not the same. I need 3-D fashion that I can touch and try on and even smell. I need fashion that's *alive*."

"Last I checked, honey, none of my sweaters had heartbeats," said Rachel's mom.

Rachel shook her head.

"Something that's not *technically* alive can still have life in it," she insisted, climbing out of the car. "Even a soul. You'd be surprised, Mom."

Her mom shook her head in confusion, then gave her daughter a loving smile.

"Trust me, Rachel," she said. "You surprise me all the time."

Usually, during her walk to homeroom, Rachel enjoyed people's reactions to her — or at least to her outfits. Her clothes always left a wake of raised eyebrows. Sometimes people called out things like "Whoa, that outfit is *crazy*."

Or "Rachel, I feel kind of dizzy just looking at you."

Or there was the ever-popular "Your clothes are so mismatched, they kind of match!"

This was the Slayton Middle School version of a compliment. About half the students in Rachel's tiny school were farmers' kids, and the rest just dressed like they were. They wore jeans and sweatshirts in the winter, cutoff jeans and T-shirts in the summer. The few who did care about clothes usually assembled outfits that looked like a window at the Gap — nice, but generic. Rachel's classmates may have been accustomed to her wildly creative looks, but they were still bewildered by them.

Today, Rachel couldn't enjoy her friends' stares, even though she was particularly proud of the new dress she'd made out of zigzaggy yellow-and-plum fabric. She was too depressed about today's terrible fashion news.

To top it all off? When she got to homeroom a few minutes before the bell, there was another horror story waiting for her.

No, really. It was an actual horror story. Luke Victorson was telling it to a dozen kids crowded around his desk.

"And then," Luke said as Rachel tossed her hand-embroidered messenger bag onto her desk, "out of nowhere, someone grabbed me!"

The room filled with gasps.

"He was behind me, so I couldn't see him. I could only feel his fingers digging into my shoulders," Luke went on. "I spun around and there was this guy with skin as white as chalk and a face like this."

Luke growled, looking about as menacing as a sandy-furred puppy.

"And you guys, his *teeth*," Luke said breathlessly. "They were black! Rotten. It was completely gross. I think he was . . . *a zombie*."

Someone laughed nervously, but the rest of the room went anxiously quiet.

Until Rachel spoke up.

"Of course it was a zombie," she said. She pointed at Luke, her eggplant nail polish glinting in the classroom's harsh overhead lights. "You were at the *haunted house* at the county fair. I went, too."

"So did I," said Olivia Hooper.

"Me too," said Megan MacEvoy. "Who am I kidding? We all went. I mean, what *else* was there to do this weekend?"

Rachel sighed.

Megan was so right. Slayton, Iowa, was a speck of a city surrounded by miles of very flat farmland. The town consisted of four sleepy streets filled with antique stores, old-fashioned beauty parlors, and the kind of boutiques that sold Wellington boots and plaid shirts instead of skinny jeans and sunglasses.

Slayton's sole movie theater had a single screen. Its only diner had been serving the exact same food from the exact same yellowed menu for the past fifty years.

So every time *something* happened in Slayton — whether it was a school play, a corn maze, or the annual county fair — *everybody* went.

Rachel had felt giddy at the prospect of something different to do that weekend. And the haunted house had been the best part. It had been filled with zombies lurching around in grisly makeup and tattered wigs, groaning and clutching at visitors.

But of course, they weren't really zombies, Rachel thought with a sniff. *They were actors pretending to be zombies.*

That's why Luke's story was ridiculous. Then again, his tall tales always were — he was famous for it.

That didn't stop several of the kids from hanging on his every word.

Chapter Two

Olivia was the first one to question Luke's I-almost-got-eaten-by-a-zombie story.

"Isn't actually touching people in the haunted house, like, against the rules?" she asked, her round green eyes getting rounder. "All the actors I saw in the haunted house *pretended* to grab me, but none of them actually did it."

"It's *totally* against the rules," Luke confirmed. "This guy went rogue. Plus, his makeup was *way* better than the other zombies. Which was why I was all, 'Maybe he's not just a haunted house employee. Maybe he's a real zombie and these are my final moments.'

"I mean," Luke went on, "what better way to feast on a lot of nice, *fresh* flesh than to *pose* as a zombie in a haunted house? Brilliant? Am I right?"

"You are right," Jeremy Shay said, twisting in his seat near the front of the classroom. "Which is why he *wasn't* a zombie. Zombies *aren't* brilliant. They're brain-dead. And, well, everything-else-dead."

"If you want more proof," Rachel piped up, "just look around. We're all still here. If any of those monsters had been real, at least one of us would have gotten eaten, right? And besides, I know which zombie you're talking about, Luke. He was wearing brand-new Nikes and a hoodie with orange and lime chevrons. His hair was waxed to perfection. I really don't see a zombie being that into fashion."

"Rachel," Luke said, "I was fighting for my life, and *you* were looking at my killer's shoes?"

"If you had *actually* been fighting for your life, I wouldn't have looked at your killer's shoes," Rachel promised him. "I would have been running in the other direction!"

Everybody laughed.

Rachel did, too. Then her classmates quieted down to finish homework, do some last-minute lip glossing, or whisper weekend gossip into one another's ears. This left Rachel with nothing to do but get broody again.

With the fair over for another year and the mall

closing, she felt she didn't have *anything* to look forward to.

I guess there's Halloween, she allowed. *It is pretty much my favorite holiday. But that's a whole two weeks away. What are the odds of anything interesting happening between now and then?*

Sighing, she pulled her sketchbook out of her messenger bag and did some shading on a pair of pants she was designing. As she almost always did when she sketched, she imagined her crisp, long-legged garment on a fashion model — an impossibly tall, willowy woman whose look couldn't have been more different from Rachel's own.

Rachel was *not* tall or willowy. She was just under five feet and had the solid, muscular build of an athlete. Her favorite way to unwind — besides sewing — was running or biking along Slayton's endless, flat, dirt roads.

Rachel also didn't think she had a model's fascinating face. Instead, hers was rosy-cheeked and shaped like a heart. Her upturned nose was sprinkled with freckles. Even with her edgy outfits, her collection of hair extensions, and as much black eyeliner as her parents would allow (which wasn't very much), Rachel couldn't escape the fact that she looked corn-fed and cute. So all her fashion fantasies featured someone *else* wearing her clothes.

As she sketched now, she could almost hear glamorous people lining a fashion runway *ooh*ing and *aah*ing over her fabulous design. That was probably why she didn't hear the classroom door opening. She also didn't see Ms. Edwards, the principal, ushering someone through it.

"Class?" Ms. Edwards said loudly. Finally, Rachel glanced up with dim interest.

"The seventh grade has a new student."

Now Rachel snapped to attention. A new student?! That was huge news!

When Rachel got a glimpse of the new kid — a girl lurking shyly behind the principal — she gasped!

Hiding behind Ms. Edwards wasn't very effective for the new girl. She was so tall that Rachel could see her entire face. It was a face that was straight out of Rachel's high-fashion daydream!

She had a jutting jawline and dramatic cheekbones with shadows beneath them. Her eyes were large, almond-shaped, and very dark under brows that were so dramatically thick, they almost looked tangled. Her hair, too, was black. It hung around her skinny shoulders in lank pieces, each of which seemed to be a different length.

The darkness of her hair made her skin look even more pale than it actually was — which was pretty darn pale. It had a blue cast to it that reminded Rachel of skimmed milk.

"Meet Lily Hack," Ms. Edwards announced. "She's here from . . . where did you say it was, dear?"

Ms. Edwards, who was not much taller than Rachel, gazed up at the new girl — Lily.

"South of here," Lily said. Her voice sounded scratchy and sleepy, as if it was the first time she'd spoken since waking up that morning. Rachel had had days like that. If she was the new kid at school, she imagined, she'd definitely be too nervous to talk much.

Of course, being a new kid at school was something that stretched Rachel's imagination. Like most of the kids at SMS, she'd lived in Slayton her whole life.

"South of here . . ." Ms. Edwards said encouragingly. She clearly expected Lily to elaborate.

But Lily didn't. Without another word, she stepped out from behind the principal and walked across the room to an empty desk. She flopped into it and gazed out the window.

As Lily did this, Rachel noticed two things:

Lily had the same loping, knock-kneed gait as a runway model. Rachel knew from watching dozens of fashion shows on YouTube.

Also, Lily's clothes were a train wreck. Her smudgy-looking waffle-weave shirt was too big, her leggings were full of holes, and her miniskirt looked like a rag that had been cinched around her waist.

Actually, Rachel realized, squinting across the room at Lily's outfit, she was pretty sure that skirt *was* a rag. It seemed to be fastened with nothing more than a messy knot.

Rachel wasn't the only one who noticed.

"So . . . Lily," said Megan, who was sitting next to the new girl. "What kind of last name is Hack?"

Lily turned away from the window, and for a moment, her eyes looked blank and her face slack. But then she seemed to give herself a little shake and crunched her face into an awkward smile. It looked as creaky as her voice sounded, as if she wasn't used to smiling very often.

"It's my favorite hobby," Lily said matter-of-factly.

She made a chopping motion with her forearm.

"Ohhhh-kaaaay," Megan said slowly. Rachel tensed, wondering if Lily would sense the mockery in Megan's tone.

But Lily seemed chill as ever. Then another kid — Jeremy — lobbed a question at her.

"So where do you live?" he asked.

Now it was Lily who raised her eyebrows, a move that clearly meant *Duh!*

Rachel grinned. The new girl had spunk! She clearly didn't feel the need to impress any of them. She had the kind of confidence Rachel would *never* have if she hadn't known all these people since she was in diapers.

"Slayton," Lily said. "I live in Slayton. That's why I'm here — at Slayton Middle School?"

"Yeah, I know," Jeremy began, "but where *in* Slay —"

He was cut off by the bell.

When it jangled loudly through the room, everyone popped out of their desks and gathered their stuff for first period. Everyone except Lily.

Rachel noticed that the new girl looked — not startled exactly . . .

Confused, Rachel realized. *She looks like she has no idea what to do next.*

She also had no stuff to gather. No backpack, no notebooks, not even a pencil.

Rachel waved at Lily.

"Hey, Lily," she said. "If you show me your schedule, I'll walk you to your next class."

Lily dug beneath the "waistband" of her raggedy skirt and pulled out a piece of paper. It already looked crumpled and dingy, even though she must have had it for only a few minutes. She handed it to Rachel, who squinted at it.

"Oh, perfect," Rachel said. "Your next class is with me — English. I'll walk you there. My name's Rachel, by the way."

Lily didn't smile or say thank you. But she did follow Rachel out into the hallway and toward the English wing. Lily was so tall and leggy that Rachel had to take two steps for every one of hers.

Good thing she walks so slow, Rachel thought, again taking in Lily's languid, loping gait.

"This school is kind of a maze," Rachel said with a smile. "Just give it six weeks or so and you'll figure it out."

Lily shrugged.

"Okay," she said. "I might still be here in six weeks."

Rachel laughed nervously.

"Um, that was a joke," Rachel explained. "Really, you should have the lay of the land by the end of the day."

"Oh," Lily said. "That's better."

She smiled. This one seemed more genuine than the grimace she'd given Megan in homeroom. Even though Lily's lips were so chapped that smiling looked painful, and even though her teeth needed some serious orthodontia and a whitening tooth-paste, the smile lit up her pale face.

Rachel felt a zing. The glamorous, mysterious, and appealingly weird new girl liked her!

"Hey," Rachel said just before they walked into the classroom, "do you want to come over to my house after school today? I could fill you in on SMS. You know, who's cool and who's nice and who's likely to Instagram you on a horrible hair day."

First, Lily looked at Rachel in confusion and said, "What's Instagram?"

But then — she said yes.

Chapter Three

On the bus home from school, Rachel was careful to choose a seat for herself and Lily in the front. Most of the other seventh graders sat in the back, and Rachel wanted a chance to chat without her nosy classmates horning in.

Lily gazed out the open window at the endless rows of corn that lined the road.

"Is it very different here," Rachel broached, "from where you came from?"

Lily shrugged.

"The last place we lived had chicken farms instead of corn farms," she answered. "So, you know, it smelled a lot better there."

Rachel breathed in the fresh, green scent of the cornstalks and frowned in confusion.

"I've been in plenty of chicken coops and they smell awful!" she blurted. "Those must have been some fancy chickens!"

Lily bit her chapped lower lip and said, "Um, yeah, I meant it smells better here, not there. *That's* what I meant."

Rachel laughed as she dug into her backpack. She pulled out a round, pink tube.

"Do you want some ChapStick?" she offered.

"Okay," Lily said, taking the tube and looking at it curiously. She didn't make a move to put any on.

Oh, no, Rachel thought. *What if she's offended that I noticed how wrecked her lips are?*

"The air here is so dry," Rachel pointed out quickly. "My lips are always really chapped. So, that's why . . ."

She pointed at the ChapStick, still lying in Lily's palm.

"Oh, I get it," Lily said. She pulled the top off the ChapStick tube and twisted the dial until the waxy stick was about an inch long.

Then she *bit* off the nub of ChapStick and chewed enthusiastically.

"My lips feel better already," she said to Rachel.

"Ummmmm." Rachel gaped at her beheaded ChapStick. "You know what? You can keep that one. I've got more at home."

Lily smiled and took another nibble of the lip balm.

The bus dropped the girls off right in front of Rachel's house.

"That's the benefit of living in farm country, where every house is, like, acres apart," Rachel joked. She opened the front gate of the white picket fence for Lily. "We get door-to-door service."

Lily stared up at the house, her mouth agape.

"Your house is *huge*," she rasped.

Rachel cringed and followed Lily's gaze. Her home was a pale blue, two-story farmhouse with cozy-looking gables, a wraparound front porch, and a brass weather vane on the roof.

Rachel had never thought of her house as *huge*, but she guessed it would look pretty nice to a girl who came to school in a rag skirt.

"You know, it *is* too big for all the time I spend alone here," Rachel said as she pulled her key out of her backpack. "My dad's the principal at the elementary school and my mom's pretty much the town's only doctor. They both work a lot."

When Lily didn't answer, Rachel chattered on nervously.

"Don't get me wrong," she said. "My parents can be total helicopters. In fact, I have to text them every day when I get home from school. It's *so* lame."

After dashing off a quick note to her parents, Rachel offered her phone to Lily.

"Do you need to call yours?" she asked.

"My parents aren't exactly worriers," Lily said drily.

Rachel led Lily to the kitchen, and peeked into the fridge.

"Ooh! Score!" she exclaimed. "Chocolate pudding!"

Rachel pulled her favorite dessert from the fridge shelf and turned to grin at Lily. But Lily was busy digging around in the fruit bowl on the counter.

"Oh, you want fruit? Well, I guess that leaves more junk food for me!" Rachel joked.

Lily ignored Rachel. She was pulling shiny green apples and bright, plump oranges out of the bowl and tossing them aside. She seemed to be hunting for something at the bottom of the bowl.

As she did, she made a low moaning sound.

Oh my gosh, Rachel thought, biting her lip. *Maybe Lily is* really *hungry. As in, needing more than an after-school snack.*

"You know what?" Rachel said. "Forget the pudding. I want a sandwich. A nice big turkey and cheese sandwich with lots of mayo. And maybe some chips on the side. Can I make you one, Lily?"

Once again, Lily didn't answer her. But it did seem that she'd found a piece of fruit she liked.

A banana.

A banana that was so overripe it was black! When Lily peeled it, the skin fell away in slimy ribbons. And what was that white fuzzy stuff Rachel spotted on the fruit? Was it *mold*?

"Lily, no!" Rachel cried out.

But it was too late. Lily had just taken a huge, slimy, fuzzy bite of the rotten banana.

"Mmmm!" she said again, but this time it was with pleasure.

"You . . . you like that?" Rachel asked.

"Yeah," Lily said, taking another big bite. "Of course. I hate underripe fruit, don't you?"

"Um . . ."

While Rachel searched for words, Lily glanced back at the fruit bowl.

"Ooh!" she said. "This one is even better."

The next banana she pulled out of the bowl appeared to have been sitting in a puddle of slime.

Rachel put a hand over her suddenly queasy stomach as Lily gobbled up the rotten fruit.

"On second thought," Rachel said weakly, "maybe I'll skip that sandwich. The pudding, too."

She rinsed the banana goo out of the fruit bowl while Lily licked her fingers happily.

"What do we do now?" Lily asked.

There was a new lilt in her scratchy voice. Her big, black eyes seemed to have an uncharacteristic sparkle in them as well. She looked happier and brighter than she had all day — which made her worn, colorless clothes seem all the drabber.

"Lily, come upstairs," Rachel proposed. "There's something I want to show you."

Chapter Four

"I look like I stuck my finger in an electrical socket," Lily said.

She was gazing into the full-length mirror on Rachel's bedroom wall. She was wearing a bright pink tank top that gave her skin a hint of rosiness, and a tutu-style skirt made with layers and layers of black tulle cut into spiky points.

"No, you look like a fashion model," Rachel corrected her.

"Okay, I look like a fashion model who stuck her finger in an electrical socket," Lily said. She poked curiously at her enormously poufy skirt, causing the gapping waistband to slip down her hips.

"Let me fix that," Rachel said, grabbing her

pincushion from her sewing table. She tightened Lily's waistband and pinned it in place.

"Wow, it's a lot easier to do that on someone else than on myself," Rachel said giddily. "Now, to accessorize!"

"Ax-what-orize?" Lily asked.

"You'll see," Rachel said mischievously.

She started by wrapping yellow satin ribbons around Lily's wrists, crisscrossing them like the ties on ballet slippers. Then she draped silver and jet-black beads around Lily's neck.

"Okay, I *cannot* reach your head to do your hair," Rachel said, gazing up at Lily. "Sit here."

She pointed at the little stool in front of her vanity. Obediently, Lily plunked herself down. Rachel started to comb out Lily's hair. Within a few seconds, the comb got stuck in a massive tangle.

"Eek, am I hurting you?" Rachel asked.

Lily just shrugged as she picked up a bottle of pearly green nail polish and watched the liquid glimmer in the light.

Rachel decided to forgo the comb and just pile Lily's hair on top of her head in a stylishly messy bun.

"Wow," Rachel said as she began to poke bobby pins into the bun. "You totally look like Audrey Hepburn."

"Who?"

"You know, Audrey Hepburn," Rachel said breezily. "She was a big movie star, and a total fashion icon, like fifty years ago. My mom ropes me into watching old movies with her sometimes. Often, they're kind of dorky, but the Audrey Hepburn ones? I could watch those over and over. Who's your favorite movie star?"

"Um, I don't really like movies," Lily said. But instead of acting cool and disdainful, she looked a bit mournful.

Again, Rachel kicked herself.

How can I be so insensitive? she thought. *Movies are expensive! I bet Lily can't afford to do stuff like that. She might not even have cable!*

"Hey, I have an idea," she said, as she put another bobby pin into Lily's bun. "We could have a movie night at your house! I could come over on a Sunday. That's the best time to find old flicks on the local channels. I could teach you and your mom how to make pop-s'mores. That's a s'more with salted popcorn tucked inside. It sounds gross, but believe me, it's the best movie snack ever. My mom discovered it accidentally one night after she tripped on her way to the couch."

Rachel giggled at the memory.

Clearly, Lily didn't get the joke. In fact, her black eyes narrowed and she curled her chapped upper lip.

"I *said* I don't like movies," she growled.

"But this isn't just about the movie," Rachel assured her. "It's about doing goofy mom-bonding. And did I *mention* the pop-s'mores? Trust me, you'll love it."

"We don't have people in my house," Lily snapped.

"Lily," Rachel insisted. "If you're embarrassed that your house might be smaller than mine or whatever, *please* don't be. I so don't care about stuff like that."

Lily's sneer softened and the angry crackle left her eyes. She cocked her head as she gazed at Rachel's reflection in the vanity mirror.

"I know you don't," Lily said.

"So we can do the movie night?" Rachel asked gleefully. "I'll bring all the food. And hey, your dad can watch with us if he wants. My dad usually flees to the garage to mess around with his tools during our movie nights, but . . ."

"Rachel?" Lily said, her eyes going squinty again. "Not a chance."

"Oh," Rachel said, feeling her face go hot. Had she pushed too hard? Was Lily going to storm away?

"Even though," Lily continued, "it does sound nice. Movies . . . moms . . ."

Pain flickered across her face as her voice trailed off.

Rachel couldn't stop herself from asking, "Lily? Is everything . . . okay? At home? Do you want to talk about it?"

Lily bit her lip. She gazed into her lap. She sure *looked* like she wanted to talk. But when she met Rachel's eyes in the mirror again, she shook her head.

"Everything's fine," she said. "It's just that — my mom doesn't like movies either."

"Oh," Rachel said carefully. "Okay. I get it."

But, as she got back to the business of Lily's Audrey Hepburn bun, she wasn't quite sure that she did.

About fifty bobby pins later, Rachel decided to finish Lily's look with some bright pink lip gloss.

"Now this you don't eat," she said, grinning as

she reached for the tube of gloss. She was just about to dab some on Lily's chapped lips when Lily batted the gloss out of her hand! The spongy applicator hit the mirror, leaving a sticky blotch that looked like a wound.

"Hey!" Rachel exclaimed.

"Oh!" Lily said, her huge eyes going even wider. "Oh, sorry."

"Why'd you do that?" Rachel asked.

"I, uh, I just don't feel like using lip gloss," Lily said.

Then she looked into her lap again.

"Um, okay," Rachel said, confused. "Would you rather paint your nails? I know you liked that green, but I have a yellow polish that would look awesome with this outfit."

Lily looked down at her nails. Like the rest of her fingers, they were bluish. Each cuticle looked raw and ragged.

"Better not," she said, sounding a little miserable.

But then, she spotted something on the vanity — a tuft of bright orange poking out of a small jewelry box.

"Oh, that's one of my hair extensions," Rachel said. "It's kind of my signature."

Lily flipped open the box and gasped at Rachel's

collection of slithery fake hair. There were lime-green braids and bright pink ringlets, stick-straight swaths of orange and zigzags of aqua blue. The only color missing was lavender, because those were in Rachel's hair.

"Mmmmmm."

Lily let out a little groan as she plunged her hand into the box. She grinned as the locks slithered through her fingers.

Then she started clipping the extensions into her hair. There was no rhyme or reason to her color choices or her placement. She poked a red strand into her bun and hooked a dark green one to her temple so it dangled across her cheek. She pinned the orange one to the top of her head and put a yellow one at the nape of her neck. It hung down her back like a tail.

"Okay, you're not looking so Audrey Hepburn anymore," Rachel said. "I was kind of going for a clean look, here."

"If you want clean, I could take a bath," Lily said. "Do you have one?"

"A bath?" Rachel sputtered. "Of course. But that's not what I meant. . . ."

Lily was turning her head this way and that, admiring the random rainbow of extensions sprouting off her head. They seemed to make her so happy that Rachel shrugged.

"Hey, have at 'em," she allowed. "After all, fashion *is* about expressing yourself."

Lily grinned and attached two more extensions to her hair — one eggplant-colored and one goldenrod.

Rachel laughed and headed for her sewing table.

"Okay, now for the big finish," she said. "The shoes. There's no way any of mine will fit your feet."

Like the rest of her, Lily's feet were long and skinny — way too big for Rachel's size fives. Luckily, Lily's own shoes were black work boots with too-short laces that left the top parts flapping around her ankles. They were a perfect, punky counterbalance to her girly outfit. Rachel just wanted to gussy them up a bit by gluing on some rhinestones.

"This will only hurt a little bit," she joked while she plugged in her hot glue gun.

"Oh, I haven't felt pain in years," Lily said with a dismissive wave of her hand.

"Yeah, right," Rachel said, laughing. "And this morning, I flew to school because I missed the bus."

"Oh, really," Lily said, nodding seriously.

"Lily!" Rachel burst out. "I'm joking. Just like you're joking?"

Lily blinked hard, then forced out a laugh.

"Ha, ha," she said. "Of course, you're right. Of course I was joking. Ha, ha. Ha."

Rachel was starting to wonder if English was Lily's second language. Maybe that was why so much of what Rachel said seemed to make no sense to her.

She decided not to ask, though. She didn't want to make Lily feel self-conscious again. And besides, she was focused on the fun of the bedazzling of Lily's boots.

"Check this out!" she said as she hot-glued pink and blue rhinestones to the ragged leather. "Bling, bling!"

After Rachel finished the rhinestones, she painted the boot's toe cap a glittery silver.

"You like?" she asked Lily, holding the boot up for her to admire.

"I love," Lily responded.

By the time Rachel had finished the second boot, the first one was dry enough for Lily to try on. Her skirt was so poufy, she had trouble bending over. So Rachel knelt in front of her and said, "Here, let me help you."

As Lily pushed her foot into the boot, Rachel spotted something on her ankle.

"Wait . . . is that *blood*?" she asked.

Lily glanced down at her leg. There was an inch-long gash on it. It looked fresh. And deep. And kind of oozy.

"Huh," Lily said, sounding completely unalarmed.

"How'd that happen?" Rachel said. "Didn't you notice?!"

"Oh, it's nothing," Lily said vaguely. "Looks worse than it is."

"Well, do you want a bandage?" Rachel asked, getting to her feet.

"Okay," Lily said with a shrug.

Rachel trotted down the hallway to her parents' bathroom and pulled out her mom's first-aid kit.

Back in Rachel's room, Lily insisted on doctoring her own wound with an alcohol swab and a roll of gauze. As she wrapped the bandage loosely around her ankle, Rachel gasped.

"Ooh, brainstorm!"

She pulled her sketchbook out of her backpack. With a few quick strokes of charcoal, she drew Lily's tall, slender figure. Then she began sketching a new outfit.

"More clothes?" Lily asked.

Rachel bit her lip and looked at her new friend.

"Do you mind?" she said. "I hope I'm not making you feel too much like a Barbie doll. It's just that you've got the *perfect* look for clothes. *My* clothes in particular."

Lily shrugged.

"Suit yourself," she said.

"That's the thing," Rachel said as she resumed her sketch. "When I suit myself, my clothes don't look nearly as amazing as when I dress *you* up."

"Eh," Lily said. "I don't think much about clothes."

"Um, yeah, I kind of gathered," Rachel said, glancing at Lily's dingy gray school clothes piled on the floor. "But you've *got* to get excited about clothes at least one day a year, right?"

"Which day is that?"

"Only the best dress-up day ever!" Rachel said. "Halloween! You know it's only two weeks away."

Rachel flipped her sketch pad so Lily could see what she'd been drawing.

"And, Lily," she said, "on October thirty-first, you are going to be Slayton's most glamorous ghoul!"

Chapter Five

On Halloween, Rachel met Jeremy, Luke, and Olivia on the town square.

"Okay, you know the drill," Jeremy said through a gruesome monster mask. You'd never know that in real life, Jeremy had floppy, dark brown hair, honey-toned skin, hazel eyes, and an ever-present, warm smile. "We hit the streets with the smallest houses. That way, we can cover more ground with more speed."

"Well, if Saturn here can keep up," Olivia joked, eyeing Rachel's costume.

"Saturn?!" Rachel squawked. Why on earth would Olivia think she was a *planet*?

"Um," Olivia said, "I just thought . . . well, you've got those big rings and all."

"I thought it was obvious what I'm dressed as," Rachel protested, giving her towering white-powdered wig an impatient pat. "I'm a deconstructed Marie Antoinette! See, I'm wearing a wide-hipped hoop skirt, but the hoops are on the *outside*. So it's kind of punk. Get it?"

"No!" Luke sputtered. "None of us ever get your crazy clothes, Rachel."

"Lu-uke!" Olivia scolded him. Then she turned to Rachel.

"*Whatever* you are," she said sweetly, "I think it's cool, especially the shoes."

"Ya think?" Rachel asked, unable to mask the pride in her voice. She'd painted the sides of her wedge soles blue and added little goldfish. "Marie Antoinette wore glass slippers with actual goldfish swimming in them. I thought this was the next best thing."

"Unless you're trick-or-treating," Jeremy complained. "Rachel, how are you going to keep up with us in those?"

"You guys," Rachel said. "It's Halloween, not a track meet."

"That's what you think," Luke said fiercely. He raised his fists, each of which was clutching a king-size pillowcase. "We have to be at the party at Jeremy's house in two hours. So that means I have a hundred and twenty minutes to fill these babies."

"Yeah, let's get going!" Jeremy said. "What are we waiting for?"

"Lily," Rachel reminded him. "She *said* she'd meet us here right at seven."

"Lily?" Luke snorted. "Like she's *ever* on time. For *anything. Ever.* The girl is so out-to-lunch, she never even makes it to the lunchroom."

"Maybe that's why she's slow," Jeremy mused. "She just needs a sandwich!"

"Hello? She needs *candy*!" Luke declared. "Let's get going! Lily'll catch up."

Rachel bit her lip. She knew *that* wouldn't happen. Jeremy knew it, too.

"Hey," he said to Rachel. "How about we pick Lily up along the way?"

Rachel shrugged. "I don't know where she lives."

"You don't?" Olivia said, looking surprised.

"Well, we've always hung out at my house," Rachel explained. "I guess her parents aren't crazy about having guests over."

"That's weird," Olivia said.

"Hello?" Luke burst out. "Everything about Lily is weird. I'm not saying I don't like her. She's cool, in a weird sort of way. But she's still, you know . . ."

"Weird," Olivia and Jeremy said together.

Rachel had to admit to herself that her friends were right. But weird or not, Rachel really liked hanging out with Lily. She loved that Lily didn't care what people thought of her, or about being late for class. She was a total free spirit.

And Lily was so patient while Rachel fitted her with outfits. She never got bored. Sometimes she stared into space and drooled a bit, but Rachel pretended not to notice.

Now, Rachel only wanted Lily to show up so everyone could see the fabulous costume Rachel had made for her.

I wonder if she even remembers that she's supposed to have a sleepover at my house tonight, Rachel thought with a frown.

"Okay," she sighed, looking at the clock on her cell phone. "It's twelve minutes after seven. I guess we better go."

"Yeah!" the boys whooped. They ran through the square.

"If you ask me, they're going a little overboard," Rachel said to Olivia as they followed the boys. Since Olivia was wearing a rotund Tweety Bird costume she couldn't do more than a waddle, and Rachel was slowed down by her towering wedge shoes.

"I don't think they're going to wait for us, much less Lily," Olivia agreed.

But when the girls arrived at the far corner of the square, they found that the boys had stopped in their tracks!

"Hey, they did wait for us," Rachel said.

But it turned out the boys weren't being polite. They were frozen in place while someone — or something — made its way toward them.

The creature was wrapped from head to toe in gauze bandages. One arm oozed green blood and dangled down by the monster's knees. Its head was a mass of bandages and black spiderwebs (complete with spiders). Its lips were black and shiny, and its teeth — seen through a ghastly smile — were green, yellow, and brown.

The monster was so terrifying, it had to be real!

Chapter Six

"Lily!" Rachel cried in delight. "You made it!"

"Hi," Lily said casually, waving at Rachel with her non-dangling arm.

Jeremy did a double take.

"*That's* Lily?" he gasped.

"Of course!" Rachel said. "Do you like her costume? I made it from scratch."

"Wow," Jeremy said, taking in the severed ear resting on Lily's cheek.

"Whoa," Luke breathed, staring at the red, beating heart glowing on Lily's chest.

"Gross!" squealed Olivia as a rivulet of black blood trailed down Lily's chin.

Jeremy turned to Rachel.

"I had no idea you had this kind of talent," he said. "You could get a job doing costumes for horror movies."

Rachel shrugged.

"I'm really more into fashion," she said. "But I figured since it was Halloween, I'd do something scary."

"It's scary all right," Jeremy said with a shudder.

Rachel felt as though she was glowing as much as Lily's fake heart. She sidled over to Lily.

"I'm so glad you made it!" she said. "You look awesome. I mean awesome in a totally grisly way. You put on your costume just right!"

"My parents helped," Lily said with a pleased little smile. (At least, it looked like a smile. It was hard to tell through all the gauze and cobwebs wrapped around her head.) "Usually, they're pretty uninterested in stuff like Halloween, but I guess something about this costume inspired them."

"Cool!" Rachel said. They fell into step behind the boys as they headed up the walk of the first house. "My parents were a little . . . confused by my costume. They were nice about it, but I think they might be happier if I dressed as something they could understand, like a vampire or a cheerleader. Bo-ring."

They arrived on the front porch, and Jeremy rang the doorbell.

"Trick or treat!" they all yelled as a gray-haired lady answered the door.

"Hi, Mrs. Campbell," Olivia said, waving politely.

"Oh," Mrs. Campbell cried. "Don't you all look just terrify —"

Her voice trailed off as her eyes fell on Lily.

"Uh, I'll just leave the bowl on the porch for you," she said in a shaky voice. "Help yourselves. Take two!"

Then, her eyes bulging with fear, Mrs. Campbell slammed the door.

While her friends dug in, Lily barely glanced at the candy bowl.

"Bo-ring," she said, using the exact same tone that Rachel had a moment earlier. Rachel laughed, but Lily was dead serious. As the group hit house after house, she continued to say no to the candy, even the king-size candy bars and Ring Pops.

She also continued to seriously creep out everyone she encountered on the sidewalk. Rachel couldn't have been more proud — but when yet another kindergartner pointed at Lily and burst into tears, Rachel realized that maybe she'd done *too* good a job. Regretfully, she suggested, "Maybe we should head to Jeremy's for the party?"

For as long as Rachel could remember, Jeremy's parents had thrown a big, post-trick-or-treating party at their house. It was one of the few things in her town that Rachel *liked* being the same every year.

And it's not just because I win the costume contest every time, she told herself as she and Lily walked to the Shays' farm just outside of town. *Although that doesn't hurt.*

Between Lily's slow, loping gait and Rachel's teetery shoes, they were among the last to arrive. When they did, the Great Candy Trade was already in full swing. Before Rachel and Lily even made it onto the big farmhouse's wraparound porch, Rachel could hear cutthroat negotiations.

"I'll give you three gobstoppers and a Bit-O-Honey for that Kit Kat," Rachel heard one boy propose.

"No way," a girl retorted.

Rachel laughed and turned to Lily.

"When will the adults get a clue?" she wondered. "I mean, has anyone ever enjoyed a Bit-O-Honey in the entire history of candy?"

Lily gave her a blank look.

"Do you *really* not like candy?" Rachel asked her. "You didn't even bother to bring a pillowcase."

"I didn't know I was supposed to," Lily said with a shrug.

"Oh, no!" Rachel said. "Is that why you didn't trick-or-treat? You should have said something. Do you want some of my candy? We can split it."

Lily shook her head, but her expression seemed to be saying something different. Were those *tears* Rachel saw welling up in Lily's big, black eyes?

Rachel reached out to touch Lily's arm (the real one, not the fake one that was dangling at her side).

"Hey, are you okay?"

"You're always so nice to me," Lily said. "You're always giving me clothes and now candy. Not that I care at all about clothes and candy —"

Rachel half gasped, half laughed.

"Gee, Lily," she said. "Tell me how you *really* feel."

"I'm trying to," Lily said. "Stop interrupting."

Rachel grinned.

"Go on," she told Lily.

"Well, someone told me once that it's the thought that counts," Lily said to Rachel. "So thanks for the thought, Rachel. If not the candy."

"You're welcome for the thought," Rachel said. "And I'm keeping the candy."

Lily laughed then. Rachel was startled to realize that that was the first time she'd ever heard Lily laugh. It sounded strange, almost like a dog barking, almost as if it was the first time Lily had *ever* laughed.

Rachel was thrilled she'd made Lily feel good enough to do it.

They climbed up the porch steps just as the candy trade was coming to a close. Everyone was chowing on candy and chattering loudly. Jeremy stood up.

"Later on, we'll vote on best costumes," he shouted, "but first — on to The Ick!"

"The Ick!" everybody yelled, clapping and laughing.

They poured through the door and gathered in the foyer outside the dining room. The room's entrance was blocked — as it was every year — by Jeremy's dad. He was dressed like a sheriff.

"Hey, that's a pretty lame costume," someone in the group complained. "You *are* Slayton's sheriff."

"Details, details," Sheriff Shay said, waving off the naysayer while the rest of the kids laughed. "Now the reason I'm here tonight is, we've got a pretty grisly crime scene in here. If you're squeamish, you might not want to come inside."

"Why, what's in there?" Olivia asked, grinning because she knew full well what was in there.

"Well, we've got a *bowl full of human eyeballs*, for one," Sheriff Shay bellowed, waggling his fingers at the group. "We've also got *bloody veins and arteries*. And let's not forget the *guts*! Still warm!"

Everybody pretended to shriek in horror. Everybody except Jeremy, that was. He turned red and rolled his eyes. Rachel gave him a sympathetic smile.

"Parents are *so* dorky, aren't they?" she said.

He grinned back at her and said, "The worst."

Rachel couldn't help but notice how straight and white Jeremy's teeth looked through his monster mask. Had he always had such a nice smile?

"So where's Lily?" Jeremy wondered.

Rachel dragged her gaze from Jeremy's sparkling teeth to look around.

"Where *is* Lily?" she wondered. She glanced around the room but before she could spot her friend, Sheriff Shay threw open the dining room doors. The room was pitch-black but for a few flickering candles. As the kids funneled into the room, they began plunging their hands into bowls of oily grapes, gushy spaghetti, and a big basin of warm, yucky pumpkin guts. They shrieked and laughed and shuddered at the wonderful grossness of it all.

"Ugh," Luke yelled. "The pumpkin really stinks this year!"

Rachel grinned as she made her way through the room. Luke wasn't kidding. The Shays had outdone themselves when it came to finding super-disgusting pumpkin innards for The Ick. Rachel could smell the funkiness as she reached the tub of guts at the end of the dining table.

She was just getting ready to plunge her hand into the squashy muck when someone else beat her to it. In the candlelit gloom, Rachel could see that the other person's hand was wrapped in dirty gauze.

"There you are, Lily," she said. "I was looking for you."

"And *I* was looking for some decent snacks," Lily said. "Something other than candy. So glad I found some. I'm starving."

Lily scooped a handful of the stinky pumpkin guts into her mouth and grinned at Rachel as she chewed.

"Yum!"

Chapter Seven

Rachel gaped at her friend through the gloom of the candlelight.

She stared at the brown-orange strand of rotten pumpkin stuck to the gauze bandage on her chin.

At the stinky squash slime on her fingers.

At the gleam of satisfaction in her black eyes.

"Lily!" she whispered. *"How can you eat that stuff?"*

Lily was too busy smacking her lips to answer. Then, a blast of vintage music came from the living room.

"Music!" Lily said with a grin. "Let's dance!"

"Dance, Lily?" Rachel said. "You?"

Rachel couldn't quite imagine Lily — with her clumsy limbs and her sluggishness — going crazy on a dance floor.

Then again, Rachel thought, feeling queasy as she stared at the pumpkin guts, *Lily is full of surprises.*

Rachel wasn't sure why she should find spoiled squash more disturbing than the other strange things Lily liked to eat. Maybe it was because she looked so creepy in her Halloween costume.

Or maybe it was because Rachel was starting to get a funny feeling about Lil —

"Come on!"

Rachel was yanked out of her thought — literally — when Lily dragged her out of the Ick room and into the living room. The chairs and sofa had been shoved against the walls, and kids were dancing to the "Monster Mash."

Lily plunged into the middle of the throng and began thrashing around. She looked completely gawky and strange, especially in her ghoulish costume.

But she also looked . . . happy. Her dark eyes had lost their sleepiness, and her gauze-wrapped face was scrunched into a grin.

After getting to know Lily for the past two weeks, Rachel knew that happiness was not an emotion she felt very often. How could she kill her friend's mood by telling her that stinky pumpkin wasn't a normal party snack?

Or that it was strange that Lily was clueless about something as basic as trick-or-treating?

Or that her spazzy, awkward movements weren't *really* dancing?

Rachel couldn't bear to tell Lily any of those things.

So she just joined her on the dance floor and started thrashing around herself.

Because it was Thursday, a school night, the party broke up early. Rachel called her dad for a ride. As they waited for him to arrive, the girls slumped against the Shays' white picket fence. Lily looked so tired, she could barely keep her eyes open. Her brief burst of energy was clearly over. But she did murmur something, so softly that Rachel had to lean over to hear her.

"Five songs," Lily said.

"What do you mean?" Rachel replied.

"That's how long you danced with Jeremy," Lily said.

"What? I didn't dance with Jeremy! I don't think you can technically dance with someone else unless there's a slow song. And there were no slow songs the whole night."

"Uh-huh," Lily said drily.

"Seriously, Lily!" Rachel insisted. "All that happened was that Jeremy danced. And I danced. Maybe we even danced sort of near each other. But we definitely didn't dance *with* each other!"

"For five songs," Lily added, her sleepy face going sly.

"For *any* songs," Rachel insisted. "It was a *group* dancing situation, Lily."

"Okay, it was a group dancing situation," Lily agreed.

But her sleepy eyes flickered for a moment — with mischief.

She thinks I danced with Jeremy? Rachel said to herself. *Forget eating rotten food and coming to school in rags.* This *is the weirdest idea Lily's ever had.*

After they got to Rachel's house for their sleepover, the tired girls headed straight upstairs. As they climbed, Rachel kicked off her teetery shoes, and Lily began to unwrap her yards of gauze.

Only when they walked into Rachel's room did Rachel notice that Lily hadn't brought an overnight bag with her. And really, she barely noticed. Of *course* Lily didn't have an overnight bag. She never seemed to bother with things like that.

I guess I'm getting used to Lily and her kind of weird ways, Rachel realized.

"I'll get you something to sleep in," she told Lily, shedding her big hoop skirt as she walked over to her dresser. She opened a drawer and pulled out a wad of nightclothes.

"That was such a fun night, wasn't it?" she chattered.

"Mmmmm," Lily said.

"Okay, granted," Rachel agreed, "my costume was kind of a flop. But *you,* Lily. You were my master-piece. Nobody else had a *chance* at winning first prize in the costume contest. People really thought you were a monster! A creepy, ooky, oozing, undead monster. Ha!"

Rachel waited for Lily to laugh at such a ludi-crous idea.

Instead, she just made a gasping sound.

"Okay, okay, I know you're wiped," Rachel assured her. "Oh, good, here are the pajamas I was look-ing for."

Holding a bundle of pink flannel, Rachel turned around to hand the pj's to Lily.

But Lily was in no shape to take them from her. Because apparently that fake arm that had been dangling at Lily's side all night? The one that was supposed to be part of her costume?

It was real.

It was Lily's actual arm.

And it was *not attached to her body*!

Chapter Eight

"Your . . . your . . . *arm*," Rachel gasped, so freaked out she could barely speak.

"Um, yeah," Lily said, glancing down at her arm before giving Rachel an apprehensive look. "You finally noticed."

To say that Lily's arm wasn't attached to her body was not entirely accurate. It dangled from her shoulder by a flap of skin and a few white, stringy-looking things that Rachel realized — with a stomach lurch — were tendons.

But, mostly, where the top of Lily's arm was supposed to join up with her shoulder, there was just a gaping, grisly hole.

"It happened when my parents and I were trying to attach the fake arm to my costume," Lily explained.

"My mom was making an adjustment, and I guess she pulled a little too hard."

"A *little*?!" Rachel shrieked.

"Rachel, honey?"

Rachel gasped as her mom's voice floated through her closed bedroom door from down the hall.

"Everything okay in there?"

Rachel and Lily looked at each other with wide eyes. Rachel paused for a long, long moment before she called out, "Yeah, Mom. Everything's fine."

Lily slumped over, clearly relieved.

Rachel, on the other hand, grew more tense than ever.

"You're my friend, Lily," she said. "That's why I just lied to my mom for you. But clearly, everything is *not* fine."

"Well," Lily said. "That depends on how you look at things. I mean, you can help me. That would *make* things fine."

She looked down at her bad arm, then pointed with her good one at Rachel's sewing table.

"You want me to *sew* your arm back on?" Rachel rasped, feeling queasy.

"Please," Lily said. "And don't worry, it won't hurt me at all. That's one of the benefits of being undead."

*　　*　　*

Rachel wasn't sure how she'd ended up on the floor. All she knew was that everything had gotten fuzzy after Lily had used that chilling term — *undead*. A moment later, she'd come to on her bright yellow shag rug.

Floating above her was Lily's face. She was close enough that Rachel could smell her breath. It smelled really bad. Like decay. Like roadkill. Like . . .

Death, Rachel realized.

Suddenly, her fuzzy brain snapped to attention.

Lily's undead, she thought. *As in dead but walking around! As in . . .*

Rachel flailed her limbs in an attempt to jump to her feet but found that her legs were too shaky to support her. So instead, she crab-walked backward, trying to put as much distance as possible between Lily and herself. She kept fleeing until she hit the corner of her room with a *thump.*

I'm trapped, Rachel thought, too shaken to speak. *Cornered in my room — with a zombie!*

And what did Lily do while Rachel cowered in the corner, mute and terrified?

Nothing.

She simply sat cross-legged on the floor, her bluish hands folded in her lap. She stared downward, looking incredibly sad.

"Lily?" Rachel rasped finally.

Lily looked up. Tears had made dirty trails down her white cheeks. Lily's tears, Rachel realized with horror, weren't colorless like a normal person's. A *live* person's.

They were brownish, like dirty water.

Rachel wondered if Lily's tears were the source of the sulfurous smell that had suddenly filled the room. She placed her fingers beneath her nose and breathed through her mouth to try to block out the stink.

"Sorry I'm so gross," Lily said. "It kind of comes with the territory."

"What territory is that?" Rachel asked her.

"You know," Lily said. "You've figured it out."

"I think I kind of need to hear you say it," Rachel said. "Or I'll never truly believe it."

"Rachel," Lily announced sadly, "I'm a zombie."

Rachel moved her hand to cover her mouth. If she didn't, she thought she might scream.

I should *scream,* she thought. *If Lily's a zombie, I'm in danger, right? About the only thing I know about zombies is they eat brains. Human brains. And other parts of us, too, I think!*

But the thing was, Lily didn't seem at all poised to devour Rachel.

During *all* their time hanging out together, she'd never attacked Rachel. Not even a nibble. The closest she'd come to cannibalism was eating Rachel's ChapStick.

This fact was comforting, but only a little.

"I'm sure you hate me now," Lily said, swiping at her brown tears with the back of her good hand. "I'll just go. *We'll go*. Me and my family. That's what we do when the truth comes out. We leave."

"Okay," Rachel said haltingly.

Lily lurched clumsily to her feet.

"But —" Rachel blurted.

Lily steadied herself on Rachel's sewing chair and looked at her, her thick eyebrows raised in surprise.

"Look, just let me fix your arm before you go," Rachel said.

Lily gaped in shock.

"You'd do that for me?" she said. "You're not disgusted and horrified?"

"Um," Rachel said, "let's just say I'm digesting this information. You know, sort of like a zombie does with human brains?"

Then she clapped a hand over her mouth, wishing she could take her words back. How dumb could she have been?! What if she unleashed Lily's true ghoul nature by reminding her of that whole "diet of human brains" thing?

Lily stared at Rachel.

Rachel squirmed.

Lily stared some more.

Rachel wondered what it would feel like when Lily took her first bite out of her.

And then . . . Lily did something that Rachel really, *really* hadn't expected.

She threw back her head and laughed. She laughed so hard that more brown tears ran down her face, and her dangling arm jiggled in an especially creepy way. When she was finally able to speak through her giggles, she gasped, "Rachel! That's the best zombie joke I've ever heard!"

Now it was Rachel's turn to laugh — a high-pitched, nervous laugh. It was the sound one made, she supposed, when you realized that your friend-who-happens-to-be-a-zombie *wasn't* going to rip you to shreds.

At least not yet.

"Well," Rachel said, crossing the room to get her sewing basket, "let's get started."

Chapter Nine

It turns out, hand-sewing someone's arm on takes a really long time.

By the time she'd finished stitching together Lily's veins, ligaments, muscles, and strangely cool white skin, Rachel's eyes were burning with fatigue. She was too tired to still be grossed out by Lily's arm or scared of Lily herself.

Lily, meanwhile, was too tired to go home. While Rachel stitched her up, she'd laid her head down on the sewing table. Lily hadn't been kidding about her immunity to pain. She truly didn't feel a thing as Rachel poked her full of holes with her needle and thread. In fact, by the time Rachel was finished with her arm, Lily had fallen dead asleep.

Literally, Rachel thought, laughing raspily as she snipped the last thread trailing out of Lily's skin.

She made to stab her needle back into her tomato-shaped pincushion but, with a glance at Lily's still-gruesome arm, thought better of it. She tossed the needle into the wastepaper basket. Then, after tip-toeing to the bathroom to scrub her hands for several minutes, Rachel returned to her room and finally collapsed onto her bed.

She wanted nothing more than to close her bleary eyes and fall asleep just like Lily. But every time she began to drift off, her mind filled with terrifying images.

She imagined waking up to find Lily lunging at her throat.

Or tearing off one of her limbs.

Or even just breathing on her with that stomach-turning zombie breath.

Over and over again these awful dreams startled Rachel awake until finally she gave up on the idea of sleeping. She sat up and turned on her nightstand lamp. Then she wrapped her arms around her knees, and contemplated her undead friend, who was still snoozing peacefully at the sewing table.

How could I not have known Lily was a zombie? she berated herself. *I mean, there were a* lot *of signs.*

There was her diet of rotten food and lip balm, for instance. Those things weren't brains, but they were still pretty fishy. So were Lily's blue-in-the-face complexion and the herky-jerky way she walked. All those qualities were *so* zombie.

Perhaps most telling was Lily's nonexistent fashion sense. Who ever heard of a seventh grader showing up to her first day of school dressed in dirty rags instead of a carefully selected cute outfit?

How does that happen? Rachel asked herself. Then she wondered something else.

How did Lily *happen? Did someone turn her into a zombie? Do some zombie bites turn you into baby zombies instead of dinner? Is Lily going to do that to me?*

What if she wants to be BFFs, Rachel wondered, *in the truest sense of the word? The two of us, putrefying together, forever?*

Rachel stared at Lily, racked with indecision.

Lily wouldn't really do that to me, would she? she asked herself. *She's my friend. We've had so much fun together. She even seems to think Jeremy Shay likes me, even though that's ridiculous. So why would Lily want me to be undead like her?*

Rachel really didn't know what to do. Should she wake up her parents and flee the house? Or should she give Lily the benefit of the doubt?

Rachel leaned back against her headboard.

Her head was swimming with questions. She knew what her dad would say: It's time for some research!

But there was no way she could sneak downstairs to the kitchen, where the family's only computer lived on a desk next to the refrigerator. If she tried, the house's squeaky, old stairs would wake up her parents. Or worse, it would wake up Lily.

Even if Rachel could get herself to the computer undetected, there was no way she could do a zombie search without her parents knowing every keystroke she made.

Being a school principal, Rachel's dad was ridiculously careful when it came to the Internet. In addition to their policy of keeping only one, very public computer in the house, Rachel's parents regularly inspected its browser history. They knew every site Rachel visited. If they figured out that she was doing zombie research, there was a good chance they'd ask her why.

And she had no idea what she'd say.

That left Rachel with no choice. She would have to do her research at school. She decided to pack her lunch the next morning so she could eat in the library while she looked for zombie books and surfed the Internet.

I'll pack something for Lily, too, Rachel thought as her eyes fluttered closed. *I'm pretty sure one way to keep a zombie from snacking on your brain is to keep her well fed with other stuff. I wonder what she likes besides rotten fruits and veggies? Maybe moldy cheese? Stinky coffee grounds? Slimy potato peels? Curdled milk . . .*

The only thing Rachel forgot to wonder as she drifted off to sleep was whether she would still be alive in the morning.

Chapter Ten

"Rachel! Time to wake up!"

Rachel's mother called through her bedroom door and gave it a brisk knock for good measure. "It's seven forty-five! You're running late for school."

Rachel dragged herself out of a deep sleep. Her eyelids felt like there were weights on them. Her arms were sore, too, from all that sewing.

"Ohhh," she groaned as she heaved herself into a sitting position. "I feel like death."

Suddenly, her eyes flew open and she sprang out of bed, running to her vanity.

Maybe, she thought in panic, *I feel like death because I am dead!*

Breathing hard, Rachel peered at herself in the mirror. Her cheeks were flushed, rather than ghostly white. Her eyes were still clear and blue. She didn't seem to have any bites, scratches, or gaping head wounds.

Her heart was still working, too. She could tell from the way it was pounding in terror.

"Whew!" Rachel whispered. She grinned in relief until she remembered *why* she'd been so panicked in the first place.

"Ack! Lily!" she gasped.

She spun around to see if Lily was there ... or if she was down the hall, eating Rachel's dad for breakfast.

"Whew!" Rachel said again. Lily was right where she'd left her, passed out with her head on the sewing table. At the sound of Rachel's voice, she lifted her head. Her black hair was more scraggly and knotted than ever and the stitches on her shoulder looked purplish and raw. Other than that, she seemed normal.

Well, normal for Lily.

"Good morning," Rachel quavered. It seemed like a ridiculous thing to say to someone who could kill you at any moment, but it was all she had.

"Mmmmmm," Lily moaned.

Then she shook her head slowly and tried again.

"I mean, good morning," she said. "Sometimes it's hard for me to talk and I moan instead. It's a zombie thing."

"Um, yeah, I gathered," Rachel said.

Lily smiled wanly.

"It feels kind of good to admit that," she said, "and not have you run screaming from the room."

"I take it that's happened before?" Rachel said with a wince.

"More times than I can remember," Lily said. "And I really mean that. When you're a zombie, you have a terrible memory. It's a side effect of having mush for brains."

"Um, speaking of brains . . ." Rachel said.

Lily sighed.

"I know," she said. "You're wondering if I want to eat yours."

"Not to be rude, but yeah," Rachel answered, feeling strangely guilty. "I *was* wondering that."

"The truth is, yeah, I kind of *do* want to eat your brains," Lily said, looking back up at Rachel.

Rachel gasped and flexed her muscles, ready to run for the bedroom door.

"But I won't!" Lily added quickly. (Well, quickly for her, anyway. Lily never did anything fast, which,

Rachel realized, was probably a good thing for her safety.) "Rachel, you're my friend. I would never hurt you. Or anybody you care about."

"In that case, I should tell you that I care very much about everyone who lives in Slayton," Rachel said breathlessly. "It's a small town. I know *everyone.*"

"Rachel," Lily said. "You don't have to worry. I do everything I can to not do . . . what you're thinking."

"So what *do* you eat?" Rachel wondered. "Besides, you know, black bananas and rotten pumpkin?"

"I get my lunch from the Dumpster behind the school," Lily explained matter-of-factly. "And every night, I raid the garbage behind the grocery store to bring home food for my parents. They're . . . well, let's just say they're a little more undead than I am. They need me to take care of them. That's pretty much the whole reason I go to school. For the food. That and to make sure nobody asks questions about why I'm *not* going to school."

"That's so sad," Rachel said. "So every other time you've been found out, you've had to run away?"

Lily nodded.

"Things would have gotten ugly real quick if we hadn't," Lily said. "Lasting two weeks here is pretty good, actually. It's longer than we usually get. I'm sure it's because of you, Rachel. I've . . . I've never really had a friend before. Not that I can remember, anyway."

Rachel bit her lip and tried not to cry. Lily's life sounded so lonely and sad. Not to mention gross. She hated that Lily had to go on the run again.

Or, Rachel thought suddenly, *does she?*

"Lily?" she said. "Do you really mean it? That things feel different in Slayton? Because of me?"

"Yeah," Lily nodded. "I really do."

"Then . . ."

Rachel wondered, during that pause, if she should just let Lily and her family leave town. That would surely be the safest thing to do. And then Rachel's life could go back to normal.

The thing was, Rachel hadn't been so crazy about her old "normal" life. But her life since Lily had arrived? It had been pretty fun, not to mention inspirational for Rachel's fashion designs.

Clearly, Lily liked her life in Slayton, too. Rachel hated for her to lose that. Lily didn't deserve to be an outcast. She couldn't help being a zombie.

"Lily," Rachel announced, "I think . . . you should stay. I'm not going to tell anybody your secret. Unless . . . unless you leave me no choice."

By, say, eating a human drumstick, Rachel thought, *or a puppy.*

Lily stared at Rachel in disbelief.

"Why would you do that for me?" she asked.

"Like you said," Rachel said, "I'm your friend. And you're mine."

This was the moment when most friends would exchange a sweet hug. But given Lily's appetite for human flesh, not to mention the fact that her sewn-on arm was still a little floppy, it seemed wiser to just smile at each other from opposite sides of the room.

"Rachel!" Her mother's voice was sharp as she called to her daughter from downstairs. "You've got five minutes. I don't want to have to drive you to school again. I made some waffles. You and Lily can eat them on the bus."

"Coming, Mom!" Rachel called out. She smiled as she breathed in the sweet, toasty aroma of her mom's waffles.

Then she cocked her head at Lily.

"What does that smell like to you?" she asked. "Pretty gross?"

Lily wrinkled her nose and stuck out her tongue (which Rachel couldn't help but notice was a pale, grayish color).

"Totally gross," she acknowledged.

"See, I'm getting the hang of this zombie thing," Rachel said. She headed to her closet. "C'mon, let's get dressed and see what we can scrounge up for your breakfast."

"I noticed you have a fishbowl in your living room," Lily noted, licking her lips.

Rachel froze and spun around.

"Lily!" she shrieked. "You can't eat Swimmy and Goldie for breakfast!"

Lily laughed.

"I was just kidding," she said. "Fresh fish is as revolting to me as a crunchy red apple. Yuck."

"Lily," Rachel said. "You're supposed to leave Swimmy and Goldie alone because they're *pets*, not because they're revolting."

"Oh, right," Lily said. "Of course."

Rachel found this response less than comforting, but she tried not to dwell on it too much.

Now that I know about Lily's zombiness, she told herself, *I can teach her what she needs to know about acting human. First on the agenda — family pets are off-limits. Second — she might want to start brushing her teeth every once in a while.*

Rachel was so busy thinking of all the ways she

could school Lily that she didn't give her outfit a thought. She just threw on the first items she saw — skinny jeans and a T-shirt — and whipped her hair into a quick ponytail.

Lily, with her grisly, stitched-up shoulder and not-quite-recovered arm, was more of a fashion challenge. Rachel bit her lip as she did a quick scan of her wardrobe.

"Oh, here's something that's perfect!" she said, pulling out a red tunic she'd made a few months earlier. It had long sleeves made of filmy panels that were supposed to flutter gracefully around the wrists. "This never looked quite right on me, but I bet it'll be magic on you."

Lily used her good arm to drag the shirt over her head and tug it into place.

"Wow, it looks like I made it for you!" Rachel exclaimed. "You look gorgeous, even with that crazy bed head you're sporting."

Lily glanced at her matted hair in the vanity mirror. She shrugged and picked up a handful of hair extensions from their box.

"There," she said, randomly poking a rainbow assortment of extensions into her hair. "Good enough."

Rachel laughed and dove back into her closet. She tossed some black-and-white striped leggings to Lily. When Lily put them on, the cuffs ended high above her ankles.

"*Man*, you're tall," Rachel said, yanking open her sock drawer. She pulled out some over-the-knee socks — also black-and-white, but polka-dotted. "Okay, between these and your boots, I think you'll be well covered."

The girls headed downstairs, Rachel praying with every step that her parents wouldn't be able to tell that Lily was a little . . . off.

Clearly, she hadn't wished hard enough. When they arrived in the kitchen, her mother took one look at Rachel and Lily and gave a little shriek.

"Wait, Mom!" Rachel cried, running toward her. "It's not what you think."

Unless, of course, Rachel added in her head, *you think that my new friend is a walking corpse.*

"Rachel, how can I *not* think it?" Dr. Harkness asked. "It's right there before my eyes. Am I right, Kyle?"

"I have to admit, she *is* right," Dad said. "We've never seen anything like this."

"I can explain!" Rachel cried, glancing over at Lily. It was hard to read her expression because her eyes had gone dull and her face slack. She looked drained of energy.

She looks, Rachel realized with alarm, *hungry.*

Rachel racked her brain for excuses for Lily's ghost-white skin, for her snarled mane and fetid breath and —

"Especially after last night," Rachel's dad said, interrupting her thoughts, "it's hard to understand you looking so mainstream."

"Wh-what?" Rachel stuttered.

"Your outfit," her mother said, pointing at Rachel's conservative jeggings and red-and-white striped T-shirt. "It's so . . . off-the-rack."

"You're not even wearing accessories," her dad added.

Rachel laughed loudly. Her parents had no idea that Lily was a monster. They were weirded out by *her.*

"Oh, this," she said, looking down at her very basic outfit. "I guess my mind was on other things this morning. Plus, we were in a total rush, right, Lily?"

"Mmmmm," Lily moaned.

Uh-oh, Rachel thought. *I've got to get her out of here.*

"So," Dr. Harkness said as she wrapped a couple of fluffy waffles in paper napkins for the girls, "Lily sleeps over and suddenly you're getting dressed in minutes and you're out the door in time to catch the bus? I think your new friend is a good influence on you, honey!"

"Yes, Lily, you should come around more often," Mr. Harkness said, smiling at the zombie standing in his kitchen.

Lily suddenly seemed to emerge from her stupor. Maybe it was because she'd never been welcomed so warmly. Or maybe she'd been jolted by the disgusting (to her, anyway) smell of the waffle.

Whatever the reason, Lily was able to blink away her monstrousness for a moment. Then she looked at Rachel and her parents and expressed a very human emotion.

"Thank you," Lily said.

Chapter Eleven

At noon, Rachel snuck her bag lunch into the school library. Eating while using the computers was strictly forbidden, but Rachel didn't have a choice. After nothing but an air-puffed Belgian waffle for breakfast, she was starving. She also didn't want to put off her zombie research a minute longer than she had to.

Lily *seemed* okay. She was grateful for Rachel's silence and friendship. And she'd seemed satisfied by the handful of moldy food she'd scooped out of the Harknesses' trash can on the way to the bus stop.

But that didn't change the fact that Lily was basically a character out of a horror movie. Rachel had a feeling that even the most well-meaning zombie was dangerous. But she wanted to know for sure. So she chose a computer in the corner of the library where Ms. Ratliffe, the librarian, couldn't see her. She logged into the library's network while carefully pulling food out of her crinkly brown bag.

When her lunch was arrayed before her, Rachel sighed. With only two minutes to scrounge up some food, she'd ended up with a naked slice of raisin bread, a chunk of cheddar cheese, a pear, and some corn chips.

How random, Rachel thought.

As she slapped the cheese onto her raisin bread and took a bite, she thought, *Well, let's start here: the diet of a zombie.*

She typed the words into a search engine and started clicking around. Some of the website writers seemed to know about zombies only from books and movies. Others wrote as if they believed zombies were real but had clearly never met one in person.

Rachel felt a funny kind of pride in the fact that she — and maybe *only* she — knew the truth. Zombies were real.

Pulling a notebook out of her bag, Rachel began to make a long list of facts cobbled together from all the sites. The most important ones were also the most chilling:

- Zombies' favorite foods are human organs, particularly brains. However, they're also fond of rotten fruits and vegetables and old meat. They don't like dairy products, no matter how sour. Zombies are notoriously lactose intolerant.
- Zombies are dead — or rather, *undead*. Some believe they're doomed to walk the earth until they find peace. Others think one becomes a zombie after being infected by a virus.
- A zombie bite will turn a human into a zombie. If a zombie eats you completely, though, you're no zombie. You're just dead.
- Zombies are in a perpetual state of decay. That's why they walk slowly and clumsily. If a zombie is wounded, it won't heal.
- Zombies are bad communicators, to say the least. They also stink at problem-solving. Put an obstacle like a fence in front of a zombie and it may be powerless to figure out how to get around it.
- After feeding, a zombie is at its most coherent and can sometimes even pass for human.

After scribbling a ton of notes, Rachel slumped back in her chair, feeling overwhelmed. She knew knowledge was power, but very little of what she'd found was comforting.

So Lily's either infected by a horrible virus, she told herself, *or she's a tortured soul, doomed to walk the earth. Either way, her life — excuse me —* non*life sounds horrible. It's so sad!*

You know what would be even more sad? Rachel asked herself grimly. *If Lily turned me or somebody else into a zombie along with her!*

Given that zombies' favorite foods were human organs, Rachel couldn't be confident that Lily would never kill. She knew Lily didn't *want* to eat anyone. But now she also knew that Lily wasn't always in control of herself. The zombie virus had made her brain mushy — and it was at its mushiest when she was hungry.

Lily's body was weakened by hunger also. She tended to wind down like a mechanical toy with dying batteries.

If she gets hungry enough, Rachel thought, *she might not be able to stop herself from attacking the nearest body. And usually the nearest body belongs to me!*

There was one ray of hope in Rachel's notes: Zombies were most coherent, and reasonable, after eating.

Rachel had seen evidence of this, too. Moments after feasting on rotten pumpkin at Jeremy's party, Lily had morphed from her usual slow-moving self into a dancing queen.

So, Rachel told herself, *the solution here is simple. Just keep Lily well fed!*

She knew farm kids whose families saved table scraps and old produce to feed to their pigs and chickens. It seemed easy enough.

If they can do it, Rachel thought, *I can do it, too. I'll just bring Lily a good (well, good as in* not *good) breakfast every morning.*

Happily, she took a big bite of her pear.

I could even help Lily Dumpster-dive after school, she thought, trying not to cringe at the idea of rooting around through the school cafeteria's garbage. *That way, I could be sure she has plenty of food each night. And also her par —*

"Oh my gosh!" Rachel whisper-screamed with her mouth full. "Lily's parents!"

Chapter Twelve

Until that moment, Rachel had completely forgotten that Lily wasn't the only zombie she had to worry about. Lily's parents were . . . how had Lily put it?

Let's just say they're a little more undead than I am, Rachel recalled.

She dropped her head into her hands.

Keeping one zombie's brain-eating urges at bay seemed manageable, but three?! How was Rachel supposed to deal with tha —

"Whoa, is it really that bad?"

Rachel started at the sound of a voice right behind her.

The voice of a boy.

A boy she knew.

"Jeremy!" Rachel gasped. And she promptly choked on that bit of pear in her mouth.

Now Rachel had two things to panic about — how to sustain an entire family of zombies, and how to act cool in front of Jeremy Shay with a piece of fruit in her windpipe.

Between coughs, hacks, and gasps, she wheezed, "I'm — o — kay."

"Are you sure?" Jeremy said, gazing down at her with wide eyes. "You don't sound okay. Do you want me to give you the Heimlich? We learned it in health class, remember?"

"Oh my gosh, no!" Rachel gasped between coughs. "I'm . . . fine . . . really!"

After another mortifying minute of retching and coughing, Rachel was finally able to speak again. "What are you doing here?"

When she realized how unwelcoming that sounded, she added, "I mean, don't you usually eat lunch in the courtyard?"

"Yeah, just like *you* usually eat in the cafeteria," Jeremy said.

So Jeremy knows where I eat lunch every day, Rachel noted. *That's . . . interesting.*

"I'm here because I had to return a book," Jeremy explained. "And . . . pay a fine."

"Aren't you the juvenile delinquent?" Rachel teased him. "You know what they say. It starts with overdue library books. Next thing you know, you're stealing cars."

"Har, har," Jeremy said drily. "The sad thing is, I turned the house upside down looking for this book. If only I'd found it earlier, it wouldn't even have been overdue."

"That's definitely not juvenile delinquent behavior," Rachel said with a grin. "That's totally upstanding citizen behavior."

"I know," Jeremy said, rolling his eyes and grinning. "Don't tell anyone. Anyway, I found the book this morning when my mom started packing up all the Halloween decorations. It was under the decapitated skeleton."

"Ooh, the one that glows in the dark?" Rachel said. "That's my favorite one of your parents' many, many skeletons! Great party last night, by the way."

"Thanks," Jeremy said. "Yeah, it was fun. I think my favorite part was dancing with you."

Rachel was really glad there wasn't any more

food in her mouth. She probably would have choked again.

Dancing with you.

Did Jeremy mean "you" as in the whole group? Or did he think that he and *Rachel* had been dancing together?

Just as Lily thought he and Rachel had been dancing together.

Had they been dancing together?

Rachel flashed back to the scene in Jeremy's living room. At first, the dancing *had* felt like a group thing — ninjas and cheerleaders and ghouls all jumping around in a throng.

But in the next song, Megan had danced facing Riley Bartlett, the boy she'd been going out with since the fifth grade. And Luke had positioned himself so that he was facing Maddie Gonzalez, and everybody knew that he had a massive crush on her.

So when Jeremy and Rachel had danced facing each other, had it . . . *meant* something?

Rachel was starting to think that maybe it *had*.

She was also starting to blush. But before she could give the matter any more thought, Jeremy pointed at her computer screen.

"Zombies, huh?" he said. "Why're you looking at that?"

Now Rachel was *really* blushing. And not in a giddy, likestruck way either. This was a panic-stricken, my-plan-to-protect-Lily-might-be-blown-before-it's-even-begun kind of blush.

"Oh, um, zombies, yeah," she stammered, glancing at the website she'd just been reading. Of course, it *would* be one that featured a movie zombie at its stereotypical worst — rolling yellow eyes, stiff outstretched arms, pointed teeth and all.

"I was looking at this page for . . ." — Rachel stalled as she grappled for a good excuse — "for . . . fashion reasons, of course."

"Fashion?" Jeremy said, his eyebrows raised skeptically. "That dude doesn't look very fashionable to me."

"I know . . . that's the point!" Rachel said. "It's . . . goth! I hear it's coming back this season."

"Goth, huh?" he said, looking again at the zombie picture. "Looks like rags to me."

"I know," she said, quickly hitting the CLOSE button to whisk the site out of view. "This one's not right. I'm looking for more dark, mysterious, Victorian kind of clothes. Did you know the Victorians were fascinated by death? They took pictures of corpses and made jewelry out of their hair."

"I didn't know that about Victorians," Jeremy said. "How weird."

"Oh yeah," Rachel said casually. "They were really dark and twisty back then."

"That's pretty cool that you know that," he said. "I'm the worst at history."

"Oh, please," she admitted. "I only know that because my mom made me sit through this boring PBS documentary about Queen Victoria."

Jeremy laughed so loud that Ms. Ratliffe stood up to shush him from across the library.

Jeremy shushed — and grinned at Rachel.

She grinned back at him.

All that grinning felt so nice that Rachel temporarily forgot about her zombie problem. She forgot she had any problems at all — until Ms. Ratliffe turned her attention on *her*.

"Rachel Harkness," the librarian barked. "Is that *food* I see in my library?"

"Oh!" Rachel squeaked, scrambling to stuff her lunch back into its paper bag. "Yes, Ms. Ratliffe. I'm sorry."

"I'm very surprised, Rachel," Ms. Ratliffe said, scrunching her thin lips into a disapproving frown. "I've never known you to break the rules in my library."

"Who's the juvenile delinquent now?" Jeremy muttered to Rachel. She slapped her hand over her mouth to suppress a snort of laughter.

Then she choked out, "I promise it won't happen again, Ms. Ratliffe. I was just so excited to do this research. . . ."

"Well . . ." Ms. Ratliffe allowed, her mouth unscrunching, "I suppose that's forgivable. Just make sure I never see you eating in here again."

"Yes, ma'am," Rachel said as she headed for the library door. "I promise."

Jeremy was right behind Rachel as she hurried out of the library. They speed-walked down the hall until they were a safe distance away. Then they burst out laughing.

"You were so busted," Jeremy said.

"And my lunch was so lame," Rachel said, clutching her stomach, "it wasn't even worth it!"

"That *was* a pretty pathetic lunch," Jeremy agreed.

"I was in a rush this morning," Rachel explained. "Too much late night, er, Halloween candy."

"I hear ya," Jeremy said. "I could barely eat my lunch. In fact, I was saving this for later, but . . ."

Jeremy reached into his backpack and pulled out half of a turkey sandwich neatly sealed in plastic wrap.

"Do you want it? I wouldn't want you to spend the afternoon undernourished."

Jeremy used a jokey tone, but it didn't change the fact that his offer was very sweet.

"Thanks," Rachel breathed, taking the sandwich from him. Just as she did, the bell rang.

"Of course, now I'm going to get in trouble for eating in *class*," she joked.

"Hello, you made a costume with a *glowing, beating heart* on it," Jeremy said admiringly. "I think you can handle something as simple as hiding a turkey sandwich behind your notebook."

"You really do want to turn me into a juvenile delinquent!" Rachel teased.

But as soon as she left Jeremy to head to her next class, Rachel's smile faded.

I wonder if he would still think I'm so clever, she thought, *if he knew I was scheming to keep a family of zombies in our town.*

Chapter Thirteen

During the break before the final period, Rachel found Lily at her locker.

"So what's your next class?" she asked.

"Musical theater," Lily said.

"Oh, that's on the way to my next one, history," Rachel said.

"Okay," Lily said, turning left and heading down the hallway.

"Aaaand it's this way," Rachel said, taking hold of Lily's arm and turning her friend around. "Hey, I've been meaning to ask you. How the heck did you end up in that class? I mean, the musical theater kids are so peppy and shiny. And you're, well, not."

Rachel knew by now that Lily would take no offense at this observation.

"The teacher loves me," Lily said frankly. "We're doing a dramatization of *From the Mixed-Up Files of Mrs. Basil E. Frankweiler*. I play the Michelangelo statue. Ms. Greene says she's never seen someone do 'inert' so well."

Rachel burst out laughing.

"I think you're really starting to fit in at SMS, Lily. In your own way."

When they arrived at Lily's classroom, Ms. Greene, the musical theater teacher, was standing in the doorway. Even though Rachel had never taken her class, she knew all about Ms. Greene. How could she not? The teacher had the kind of personality that filled every room she was in.

"Lily, *darling*!" Ms. Greene said, coming into the hallway to greet her. She grabbed Lily's hands and stretched her arms out so she could get the full fluttering effect of her sleeves.

"Another *fabulous* outfit. How *do* you do it?"

"I don't," Lily said bluntly. She pointed at Rachel. "She does. She made this."

Ms. Greene turned to Rachel, and Rachel found herself backing up a step. Ms. Greene had wild, red curls and a buxom figure. She always wore glittery eye shadow and clothes with extremely bright, busy patterns. She seemed to come straight at you, even when she was standing still.

"Rachel, isn't it?" Ms. Greene asked. "So you *made* Lily's gorgeous ensemble?"

"Uh-huh," Rachel squeaked.

"No 'uh-huh,' Rachel," Ms. Greene pronounced. "I expect excellent diction from my students."

"Sorry. Yes, ma'am," Rachel said. "But, um, Ms. Greene? Technically, I'm not one of your students."

"Oh, no?" Ms. Greene said. She arched one penciled eyebrow dramatically. "You're about to be. I assume you know about the Winter Revue?"

"Of course," Rachel said.

The Winter Revue was a show choir extravaganza, a bunch of song-and-dance numbers strung together by a theme, like movie music or the Olympics. At least half the kids in the middle school took part in it every year. The revue was held in the high school auditorium, the only place in town with enough seats for all the people who wanted to see it.

The show was so popular, Rachel thought, either because Ms. Greene's directing skills were off the charts or there *really* wasn't enough to do in Slayton. Either way, she was a big fan and went every year.

"I want you to make the costumes for one of the numbers," Ms. Greene said.

"Really?!" Rachel said. "Um, wow. That sounds amazing, Ms. Greene. But also kind of time-consuming, which is a little bit of a problem because —"

"You'll make time," Ms. Greene said, dismissing Rachel's worries with a flick of her plum-colored nails. "You're young. The young sleep entirely too much."

Rachel was pretty sure her mom, the doctor, would disagree with that, but she knew not to say anything. Ms. Greene went on.

"This year's theme," she announced, "is Music Through the Ages."

"That sounds cool," Rachel said, nodding thoughtfully.

"Cool? Cool?!" Ms. Greene said, rolling her eyes. "My dear, it will be brilliant. The parents and grand-parents will be beside themselves with nostalgia. And you children will be exposed to music with more depth and soul than your silly boy bands could ever dream of."

Rachel leaned over to Lily.

"Seriously?" she whispered. "Who listens to boy bands anymore?"

"Seriously?" Lily whispered back. "You're asking *me* that question? The zombie who doesn't have electricity, much less a radio?"

Rachel clapped a hand over her mouth to keep from guffawing.

Meanwhile, Ms. Greene was listing the songs she had planned for the revue.

"Of course," she said, "there will be Elvis and the Beatles. We will have Motown! And Bob Dylan. Grunge! Oh, and we can't forget the eighties. I'm thinking Madonna or Michael Jackson."

"Michael Jackson?" Rachel said. "*Thriller*! Oh, that's perfect."

"And why is that?" Ms. Greene asked.

"Have you ever seen the *Thriller* video?" Rachel asked. "My dad showed it to me on YouTube. Apparently, it was like this revolutionary thing way back then. All these ghouls did a big dance number and Michael Jackson turned into a zombie!"

At the mention of the Z word, Lily gave a little jump. She turned to stare at Rachel.

Rachel gave her a look that telegraphed, *Don't freak. Just hear me out.*

She pulled her cell phone out of her backpack and began scrolling through her photos.

"As you can see," she told Ms. Greene, "I'm pretty good at zombie outfits."

She held up the phone so Ms. Greene could feast her eyes on Lily in her Halloween costume.

Now it was Ms. Greene who took a startled step backward.

"My goodness," she said. "Rachel, you've got quite a talent for the macabre!"

"Thanks!" Rachel said. "So what do you think? I mean, here I made Lily into a great zombie when in real life she's just a *very* ordinary, not at *all* undead girl. So I could probably do it with other kids, right?"

"Lay it on a little thicker, why don't you?" Lily muttered, but she did it with an appreciative smile.

Rachel grinned back at her before she finished her pitch.

"An act like this would make zombies out of all of us," she said. "It would send a message. There's nothing to fear from zombies. They're just like us, only a little more, well, dead."

While Ms. Greene digested all this, Rachel felt something cold and creepy touch her hand. She jumped — until she looked down and saw that it was Lily's hand, grasping at her own.

Rachel looked up at her friend. Lily's eyes were welling with muddy tears.

"Thank you," she whispered.

Before Rachel could reply, Ms. Greene pronounced, "I love it! Rachel, you're hired. You've already got Lily's measurements, obviously. I'll get them from the rest of the cast members ASAP. You'll need to start immediately. The dress rehearsal is two weeks from today."

"Two weeks?" Rachel squeaked. "To make a dozen costumes?"

"Probably more like fifteen," Ms. Greene said breezily. "I recommend espresso to help you stay up later. It's also very good for the bones."

Rachel was *really* sure her mom would disagree with that one.

But still, she couldn't say no. She was thrilled to have her first real fashion design gig, even if the deadline was going to be a killer.

She'd also meant what she said. She thought turning a bunch of her friends into make-believe zombies could only help to spread a little peace, love, and understanding for the undead.

Maybe that would help Lily and her family survive — so to speak — in Slayton.

Chapter Fourteen

The last bell of the day usually gave Rachel a rush of freedom.

But today, it felt like the first tick of a stopwatch. As she headed for her locker, her head swam with her new to-do list.

1. Sketch costumes for 15 zombies.
2. MAKE costumes for 15 zombies.
3. Single-handedly prevent the Hack family from eating any Slaytonians.
4. Study for Tuesday's science test.

"Okay," Rachel muttered to herself while she packed her backpack, "if I simply spend the entire weekend doing nothing but working, taking breaks only to bring food to Lily and her parents, I can get a good start on the costumes."

She slammed her locker door shut, revealing Megan, who had the locker next to hers.

"Hey, Rachel," she said. "Wasn't last night epic?"

"That is definitely a good word for it," Rachel said as she and Megan began to walk toward the front door.

"I'm so glad to have a night off tonight," Megan burbled on. "But tomorrow! It's all about the last day of the corn maze! What time are you coming?"

"Um, I'm going to the corn maze?" Rachel asked, confused.

Megan's dad was a farmer. He built a corn maze before every Halloween. He used the attraction to sell pumpkins, doughnuts, and hay rides, but the star was definitely the labyrinth made of towering cornstalks. Every year the maze got bigger, more confusing, and in Rachel's opinion, scarier. To her, being lost in a maze was about as fun as being a lab rat. She only submitted to the corn maze if someone goaded her into it. She was always kind of glad when the maze was dismantled right after Halloween.

"I asked Lily if she was coming and she made this kind of moaning sound?" Megan said. "But it seemed like a happy moan, so I figured that meant yes. And since you guys have been besties since Lily got here, I assumed you were going together."

Rachel grimaced. Her research had taught her that zombies *don't* take well to obstructions or brain teasers. Which meant Lily in a maze would be an absolute mess!

So, with a sigh, Rachel told Megan, "Well, it looks like I *am* going to the corn maze. I'll just put it on my to-do list."

"Ha, you sound like my mom," Megan said.

"I kind of feel like a mom right now," Rachel muttered, thinking about all the people she suddenly had to take care of. (Well, they were *sort* of people.)

"What did you say?" Megan yelled. She and Rachel had just walked outside and the *chug-chug-chug* of the school bus had drowned out Rachel's voice.

"Oh, nothing," Rachel said. "Tell me, Megan? Have you ever drunk espresso?"

"No! Why would I?"

"That's what I used to think," Rachel said. "But something tells me I'm going to need some soon."

When Rachel climbed aboard the bus, Lily was already there, sitting in their usual seat. Her head was tipped so that it rested on the window. The sunshine streaming through it made her look more pale and ghostly than ever. For the first time, Rachel noticed that Lily had dark purple circles under her eyes and that her lips were on the blue side, too. She looked so wan and vulnerable, it was hard to believe she was capable of cracking open a human skull like a walnut.

But she is, Rachel reminded herself. *I can't forget that.*

"Lily," Rachel began, "there's something I want to do."

"What?" Lily grunted.

"Meet your parents," Rachel said.

Lily lifted her head and glared at Rachel.

"Didn't we go over this already?" she growled.

"But, Lily —"

"No, I mean it," Lily said. "Did we? I can't remember."

"Oh," Rachel said. "Oh, yeah, you made it very clear you *don't* want me to meet them. But why?"

"Because they're *so* embarrassing!" Lily said.

"Lily, *everybody's* parents are embarrassing," Rachel said. "It's part of the job description. Remember how mortified Jeremy was by his dad at the party last night?"

"Jeremy, huh?" Lily said. "Jeremy who you danced with three times?"

"Five," Rachel said automatically, before clapping her hand over her mouth. "Not that I'll admit to dancing with him. Don't try to trick me, Lily."

"I didn't," Lily said. "I'm just really bad with numbers."

"*Any*way . . ." Rachel said. Her cheeks felt hot and she was desperate for a subject change. "We were talking about your parents. And how there's nothing to be embarrassed about."

"My parents can't speak in complete sentences," Lily said. "They drool. Between the two of them, they have about seven fingers. Maybe more. I'm bad —"

"With numbers," Rachel interrupted with a sympathetic smile. "I know."

She fell silent for a moment, wondering what to say next. She couldn't tell Lily the truth — that learning where Lily lived and meeting her parents were security measures. Rachel had to know what she was dealing with. Were Lily's parents the dangerous kind of undead or just the clumsy, sluggish kind? Was their home safely in the middle of nowhere or near other people?

Now that Rachel was knowingly encouraging Lily to stay in Slayton, she knew any harm the Hacks did was on *her* hands. So, as the final part of her research, she needed to go to the source — to Lily's home. She wouldn't be able to rest easy until she did.

What with my new espresso habit, Rachel thought, *I might not be able to rest, period. But still . . .*

"Lily," Rachel said. "I've told you I want to help you and your parents make a life here in Slayton. I just want to know who I'm helping, that's all."

"I guess I get it," Lily allowed. "But you'll have to wait until later. I've got to get some food in them. Otherwise, they'll treat you like pizza delivery."

"Say no more," Rachel said with a gulp. "Tell me how to get to your place?"

"It's a long walk," Lily said.

"That's good!" Rachel burst out.

Lily gave her a sidelong glance.

"I mean, no problem," Rachel corrected herself. "I can ride my bike."

Lily described the location of her house in her own strange way.

"Then, at the house with the mean dog, turn off the hard road onto the soft one. . . ."

Only because Rachel knew her town so well was she able to figure out where Lily lived.

"Oh!" she said. "Lily, are you in that barn under the big oak tree? The one that's so destroyed, there's hardly anything left to it but the old, rusty roof?"

Lily thought for a moment, then nodded.

"It pings when it rains," she said, describing the sound every farm kid knows — the sweet *ping* of raindrops on a tin roof.

"I know where that is!" Rachel said. "That's a perfect spot. It's on a plot of land that Mr. and Mrs. Sarner are keeping wild. They say they want to give it to their grandkids one day, but since the kids are still little, you've got plenty of time."

Lily gave Rachel a skeptical look.

"Plenty of time," she harrumphed.

"Seriously," Rachel insisted. "We're going to make this work, Lily. I promise."

Chapter Fifteen

Back at home, Rachel went upstairs to pack some essentials for Lily and change her own clothes — until she remembered she was wearing a completely utilitarian (slash boring) outfit already.

"How convenient," Rachel muttered as she looked down at her jeggings and T-shirt. "If I get sprayed with rotten food or zombie slime, I'm all ready with a wash-and-wear outfit."

She tried to laugh at her own joke, but she could barely muster a giggle. Her mouth was dry and her hands were shaking.

"Maybe I'm just hungry," Rachel told herself, heading back downstairs with the bag she'd packed for Lily. "I didn't have much lunch, between my zombie research and Jer —"

Rachel stopped herself before saying Jeremy's name. She cocked her head and called out, "Mom? Dad? Anybody home?"

When no answer came, Rachel sighed with relief. The last thing she needed was her parents hearing her muttering the name of her crush —

Wait a minute! Rachel thought, screeching to a halt in the kitchen doorway. *Crush?! Since when have I ever used that word about Jeremy Shay?!*

The answer came to her almost immediately.

Since he suddenly started looking cute and giving me turkey sandwiches.

Rachel tried to shake the thought away, but it stuck fast. So did the secret little smile it brought to her face.

When she opened the fridge to search for a snack, her smile grew wider.

"Jackpot!" she said. In the clear plastic drawer of the vegetable crisper, she could see something green — a zucchini, perhaps — forgotten and buried beneath fresher produce. The green thing was slimy and coated with white fuzz.

Rachel deposited the disgusting zucchini, some shriveled corncobs, and a few other slimy veggies into a plastic bag. She also added an old hamburger that looked like a dry hockey puck, and a container of forgotten and funky canned beans. She tied a knot in the bag and set it on the counter so she could get back to finding a snack for herself.

Too bad the rotten veggies had killed her appetite.

In the end, she reached for a stomach-settling Halloween hard candy. After popping it into her mouth, she rummaged in the cabinet for the biggest Tupperware bowl she could find. She plunked it onto the counter next to the sink, then found a pad of paper and pen and wrote:

Parental units, we're doing a composting proj-
ect at school. Please put all leftover and/or bad
food in this bowl instead of throwing it out.
Anything can go in except cheese and other
dairy products. I need you to do this. My grade
(and the environment) depend on it. Thanks!
Love ya,
Rachel
P.S. Probably having dinner at Lily's tonight.
Be back by 8.

Rachel felt a little guilty for the white lies she'd written in her note.

On the other hand, she thought, *I can't say that my life depends on our little composting project, or that I'll probably be dinner at Lily's. I wouldn't want to alarm them.*

With that, Rachel gathered all her supplies, took a deep, shuddering breath, and headed out to pay her first-ever visit to a family of zombies.

Rachel didn't ride her bike toward Jeremy Shay's house on *purpose*. It was truly and legitimately on the way to Lily's.

And Rachel definitely didn't think Jeremy would be in front of his house as she pedaled by. But sure enough, there he was, oiling a hinge on the front gate.

"Hey, Rachel," he called. She stopped and smiled at him. "Where you heading?"

"I'm going to Lily's," Rachel said, trying to sound casual. After all, Jeremy had no idea that she was pretty much saying, "I'm flirting with death."

"Really?" Jeremy said. "I thought Lily wouldn't tell you her address."

"Oh!" Rachel said. "Right. Well . . . she changed her mind!"

"So?" Jeremy prompted her. "Where does she live? What's the big secret?"

"Well, it's still a secret," Rachel said. "She made me promise not to tell. I think she's a little embarrassed. You know, because her parents don't have much."

"Yeah, you can kinda tell," Jeremy said, looking troubled. "I mean, her clothes were a mess until you started giving her some of *your* crazy outfi —"

Jeremy stopped himself before he could finish the word.

"I mean," he stammered, "what I meant to say was your outfits are crazy-*cool*."

"Jeremy," Rachel said with a grin. "Don't worry. I'm not offended. I know my clothes are a little crazy. That's what I like about them. You can't succeed as a fashion designer if you don't break some rules, you know?"

"If you say so," Jeremy said, making Rachel laugh. "Anyway, the only reason I was asking about Lily is — maybe I could tell my dad about her. Being sheriff, he knows the county social worker. She could help Lily's family get food stamps or a better house."

This was both the nicest *and* most disastrous proposal Rachel had ever heard.

"Um, I have a feeling that Lily's parents might be too proud to accept help like that," she said. "You know, from what she's told me."

"Okay," Jeremy shrugged. "But just say the word if you think they need help."

As Rachel smiled at him, a sudden gust of wind ruffled Jeremy's shiny, brown hair, making him look incredibly cute. When he smiled back at her, he looked cuter still.

The moment was pretty much perfect until, suddenly, a disgusting odor swept over them. It was the kind of funky, foul smell that made you peek at the bottom of your shoes to see if you've stepped in something.

But of course, Rachel didn't have to do that. She knew that the stench had come from her! Or rather, from her bag of rotten produce. Clearly, her bike ride had jostled the plastic bag open and it was now spewing vile smells into the air.

"Oh, yuck, sorry," Rachel said, her face going pink

At the exact same time, Jeremy blushed and said, "Oh, gross, sorry."

"Wait," Rachel said, "isn't that smell coming from my bag of compost?"

She pointed at the plastic bundle in her bike basket.

"Oh!" Jeremy said. "I thought it came from my mom's cornfield."

He pointed at the field beyond his house. The cornstalks looked brown, thin, and ragged. Many of them were listing to one side. Some were folded entirely in half.

"Our combine broke over the summer," Jeremy explained. He was talking about the machine farmers use to pick their ripe corn ears, then grind the stalks into sweet, fragrant mulch. "And you know, my mom's not a big, field corn farmer like a lot of folks around here. She just grows sweet corn for farmers' markets and stuff."

"Of course," Rachel said. "We ate your mom's awesome corn all summer."

"Now, it's not so awesome," Jeremy said. "Mom didn't want to pay to have the combine fixed or to get a new one. So we picked the ears by hand and now she's just letting the stalks rot in the field. Eventually, they'll break down and fertilize the field for next season. But in the meantime, we have to live with the stink."

"Just like I have to live with the funk of this composting project I'm doing for my science class," Rachel said with a grin.

"So the big question is," Jeremy said, "whose stink are we sniffing right now?"

At the same time, both of them said, "Definitely yours."

Then they giggled madly before Rachel waved good-bye.

Okay, she thought as she rode on, *bonding about mutual bad smells has got to be the weirdest way to flirt in the history of flirting.*

But as anyone could tell from Rachel's wardrobe, or from her friend, Lily — Rachel had no problem with weird. In fact, she liked weird quite a lot.

Chapter Sixteen

Okay, Rachel thought ten minutes later, *maybe I don't like weird* this *much.*

She'd just arrived at Lily's. The structure where the Hacks were living was little more than a bent and rusted tin roof, maybe ten feet tall at its highest peak. The big, wooden barn that once supported the roof had rotted away bit by bit over the years. Now there were just a few panels of siding holding the roof up. Vines coiled out of rusty holes in the tin and the whole sagging structure looked as if it could fall into a heap at any moment.

It didn't look like a home fit for wild animals, much less a family of three, even if they were three zombies.

At the sound of Rachel's footsteps rustling through the weeds surrounding the barn, Lily poked her head through a "doorway" made of splintered boards. Seeing Rachel, she grimaced and came outside.

"So you came," she said flatly.

"And hello to you," Rachel joked, but her voice was shaky.

When two moaning, groaning voices echoed from somewhere beneath the tin roof, Rachel's knees began shaking, too.

"That's them?" Rachel asked Lily fearfully.

"That's them," Lily said.

"Is that their way of saying hello?"

"That's the sound they make when they smell food," Lily said.

"Oh, right," Rachel said. "I brought this." She lifted her bag of stinky produce out of her bike basket.

Lily shook her head and pointed at Rachel herself.

"Food," she said.

"Um, maybe we should just stay out here," Rachel quavered.

Lily nodded and reached for the plastic bag. Rachel tried not to curl her lip as Lily ripped it open, pulled out the slimy old zucchini, and devoured it. She gobbled part of the hamburger and shriveled corn, too.

With the rest of the food, she ducked inside. A moment later, her parents' moaning stopped. The fact that they were eating made Rachel feel a little safer.

But not much.

Tentatively, she moved toward the barn "door." It was dusk now, but there was enough light shining through the holes in the roof that she could see into the structure.

You'd never know that anybody lived there. The dirt floor was littered with splintered wood, broken farm machinery, and other trash. Rachel couldn't see a bed or a table or any sign of comfort except . . . what was that? Rachel thought she saw a flash of color on the left side of the slanted ceiling.

Poking her head through the door, Rachel peered into the gloom. Hanging from the low side of the tin ceiling was a row of thick, round eye hooks. They had probably once been used for a rope and pulley system that hoisted hay bales into the barn loft. Rachel had seen similar ones in friends' barns.

But these hooks were being used as . . . clothes hangers. Every item of clothing that Rachel had made for Lily had been hung carefully from a hook.

Well, Rachel corrected herself with a sad smile, *"carefully" might be a stretch*. One of the garments hung by a sleeve, another from the bottom hem. They all looked haphazard, limp, and dusty.

Anything would be dusty after about thirty seconds in this place, Rachel thought.

In each garment, Rachel saw what could have been, if Lily were a regular girl instead of a zombie. In the hot pink tank top and fluffy black tutu, Lily could have been a dancer, one whose limbs moved with grace instead of stiff, jerking motions.

And there was the bright yellow dress Rachel had given Lily, the one with orange and aqua arrows chasing each other around the hem. Rachel could just see Lily wearing it on the Ferris wheel at the county fair.

And in the cobalt-blue miniskirt and swingy, charcoal top, Rachel imagined, Lily could be sitting in the front row of a high school English class, raising her hand to say something smart about a nineteenth-century novel.

Continuing to gaze at the clothes, Rachel imagined Lily with more than one friend.

She saw her cutting her hair into a pixie cut, knowing it would grow back when she wanted it long again.

Rachel could see Lily growing up.

She could see . . . two pale, wild-eyed faces lunging at her from the gloom!

Rachel had been so absorbed in her wistful daydream that she hadn't noticed Lily's parents shuffling toward her from the back of the barn!

"Mmmmmm!" they groaned. Lily's parents had the same colorless skin, matted hair, and bottomless black eyes as their daughter. But just as Lily had said, all their zombie qualities were a bit more extreme than hers. Where Lily's skin was milky, theirs was so pale, it looked almost gray.

Their teeth were browner than Lily's and some of them were missing. And while their hair was ragged and tangled just like Lily's, it was dust-colored instead of blue-black.

Their clothes looked like filthy rags that had been wrapped around them and stapled closed. (For all Rachel knew, Lily had done the stapling.) And their hands, as Lily had warned, were missing a few digits.

They were also outstretched and reaching for Rachel!

Rachel was so scared that she couldn't move, couldn't breathe! With no air behind it, her scream was nothing but a raspy squeak.

But then Lily's mother batted at Rachel's cheek with her three-fingered hand. Her zombified skin felt so shockingly cold that Rachel unfroze. She sprang backward, ready to turn and run.

The only problem? She wasn't getting anywhere. Her T-shirt was snagged on a piece of splintered barn wood! She yanked desperately on her shirt, but that only seemed to embed the wood shard deeper into the fabric.

"Lily!" Rachel cried. Her strangled voice was still maddeningly faint. *"Lily!"*

Rachel tried to peer past the zombies into the back of the dark barn. *Where was Lily?*

"Mmmmmm!" Now Lily's father, tall and broad-shouldered, was looming over her, too. As he reached for Rachel, she finally found her voice. She shrieked so loudly that she startled even herself. *"Noooo!"*

She twisted away from the zombies, hearing her T-shirt give with a loud *riiiipp.*

She fell on her backside and began scrabbling away from the barn in a frantic crab walk.

"Lily!" she screamed. "Help!"

The Hacks were wedging themselves through the doorway, intent on catching her. They bared their teeth and growled, looking more mindless than monstrous. But a mindless zombie with an instinct for killing humans? That was terrifying enough for Rachel. She felt her skin go prickly with cold sweat. Her stomach heaved and her eyes fluttered. She was going to pass out.

She was going to pass out and these zombies were going to catch up with her and —

No! Rachel ordered herself fiercely. *Don't think about it and DON'T FAINT.*

She forced her eyes to stay open. She shook her head, trying to defog it. She flipped herself over and struggled to her feet.

And then, she ran.

Chapter Seventeen

Rachel had gotten only a few yards away when Lily appeared out of the night. She was moving faster than Rachel had ever seen her move, her black hair flying out behind her and her arms flailing wildly.

"Mom! Dad!" she cried. "Stop!"

She planted herself between Rachel and her parents, who were still shuffling their way doggedly toward her.

Lily placed a hand on each of their chests, pushing at them. Her mother batted Lily's hand away, sending one of her fingers flying.

"Aaaah!" Rachel cried. But Lily barely seemed to notice. Instead, she pulled something out of a bag that was slung around her shoulder.

"Here!" she shouted at her parents. "Here!"

It was some kind of animal — a squirrel! Before Rachel could even see if it was alive or dead, Lily's parents pounced on it. Moaning with hunger, they took it back to the barn and ducked inside to dine in the musty darkness.

Rachel's legs felt wobbly suddenly. She stumbled as far from the barn as she could, but then her legs gave out and she had no choice but to sit down in the grass. She turned herself toward the barn so she could watch for any signs of the zombies reemerging. Then, breathing hard, she put her head in her hands and tried to recover.

"Rachel."

It was Lily, walking toward her.

Rachel lifted her head and glared at her friend.

"Where were you?" she demanded. "Your parents were *this* close to —"

She stopped herself before she finished her hurtful sentence.

— *to turning me into one of you.*

"I saw that squirrel through an opening in the back of the barn," Lily said, sitting creakily on the ground next to Rachel. "I knew it would distract them from your scent so I went to get it. And then, I guess *I* got distracted. Because —"

"Because of your zombie brain, I know," Rachel said. She tried to be sympathetic, but she was still angry.

"I brought you guys food!" she said to Lily. "They just ate it! Was that not enough?"

"No, it wasn't," Lily said. "There's a reason zombies' favorite foods are brains and guts. They're way more nutritious than rotten zucchini."

"Then this is hopeless!" Rachel cried. "If they're not satisfied, how can I ever trust that they won't harm somebody. Or that *you* won't, Lily! I know you mean well, but . . ."

Lily looked down at her hands folded in her lap. If she noticed that the index finger was missing from her right hand, she didn't seem to care.

"The last thing I ever want to do is hurt you," Lily said. "I've been so careful. Remember, I wouldn't even let you put lip gloss on me because I didn't want to risk infecting you."

"So it's true," Rachel breathed. "Zombie-ism is caused by a kind of virus."

Lily nodded.

"How . . . how did it happen to you guys?" Rachel asked delicately.

Lily gazed at the barn and said, "It was my dad. He was on a business trip."

"Business trip?!" It was hard to imagine Lily's dad ever having a job or taking a plane flight. "What kind of business did he do?"

"I don't know," Lily said. "We used to have a photo album. There were pictures of my dad wearing a white shirt — so clean and crisp. My mom wore glasses. She was pretty. In one photo, she was riding a horse. In another, she had a big, round belly. I think that was me —"

Lily broke off and shook her head.

"The photo album got lost," she said. "That tends to happen when you move around a lot and nobody has much memory to work with."

"But do you know what happened?" Rachel asked gently. "During your dad's business trip?"

"He got bitten," Lily said simply. "By the time he got back home, he . . . he wasn't himself anymore, which is probably why he bit my mom. I think he's always regretted it, in his own brain-dead way."

Rachel gasped quietly and put her hand over her mouth.

"And you?" she asked.

"I wasn't born yet," Lily said. "I came along a couple of weeks later. When I did, I was infected, too."

121

"So you've been this way all your —"

Rachel stopped herself again. She couldn't say *life*. Lily had never truly been alive! Being a zombie was all she'd ever known.

"Forever, yes," Lily said, nodding as if she'd known what Rachel was thinking.

"But I don't get it," Rachel said. "How did you grow? Wouldn't you have stayed a baby forever?"

"I think because I was infected so soon before being born, there's still a bit of life left in me," Lily said. "That's why I'm not as zombified as my parents and that's why I've gotten older."

"So you *will* grow up," Rachel said, feeling new hope surge through her. "Lily, that's great!"

Lily didn't answer.

Because maybe, Rachel realized, *she doesn't think it's so great. I probably wouldn't either, unless things could change, somehow.*

The thought brought her back to the problem at hand.

"Lily," she said, "I really want to help things be better for you. But clearly my little composting project isn't going to be enough for your parents."

"No," Lily said. "But a *big* composting project would."

"I don't get it."

"We don't feel the need for brains or anything else like that," Lily said, "if we can get a *lot* of rotten fruits and vegetables. A few slimy zucchini aren't going to cut it."

Rachel slapped her forehead with her palm.

"Of course," she said. "I've been giving you guys little side salads, when what you need is a salad *bar*. With, like, bacon bits and croutons and olives. The whole shebang."

Lily smiled.

"Replace that stuff with rancid bacon rinds, moldy toast, and olive pits," she proposed, "and I like what you're saying."

"So we've just got to step up the Dumpster-diving," Rachel said determinedly. "With two of us doing it, we can get twice as much food. Do you think that'll be enough?"

"I hope so," Lily said.

Fearfully, Rachel looked at the barn again.

"Have your parents seriously never tried to break out of the barn before?" she said.

Lily shook her head.

"They prefer it in there," she said. "Only serious hunger for human flesh could lure them out. And you're the first person who's come anywhere near here since we arrived."

"I wish we could figure out how to make sure I'm the last," Rachel said. Her mind was spinning with all the problems she had to solve.

"Why would any human want to visit a place so horrid?" Lily asked Rachel.

"Good point," Rachel said nervously. "I guess that's good enough security. Until I can think of something better . . ."

Suddenly, she remembered what else she'd packed in her bike basket.

"Speaking of something better," she said, "I brought some stuff to make things a little more comfortable for you."

She handed Lily all the supplies she'd packed: a flashlight, a toothbrush and tube of toothpaste, a warm fuzzy nightgown, and some fashion magazines. There was also something Rachel had decided on at the last minute — a teddy bear that she'd won at the county fair. Even though Lily wasn't a hugger, Rachel had had a feeling that she might like something soft to cuddle.

Clearly, she'd been right. When Lily saw the bear, her face lit up. She cradled it in her arms, dug her cold fingers into its plush purple fur, and grazed its fuzzy ears against her cheek.

Only then did she notice that Rachel had clipped something onto the bear's ears.

"Hair extensions!" Lily exclaimed.

"I know you like them," Rachel said, "so I ordered a bunch more off the Internet."

Lily began trying to clip the colorful extensions in her hair, but they kept slipping from her grasp and falling to the ground.

"You know what would make that easier?" Rachel said. She pointed at a patch of dirt nearby. In the middle of it lay Lily's index finger. "All ten of your fingers."

"Will you sew it back on for me?" Lily asked.

Rachel nodded. "Why don't you come over tomorrow afternoon and I'll do it before we go to the corn maze," she said.

Lily grinned and loped off to the patch of dirt, plucking her finger off the ground as casually as someone else might pick up a lucky penny.

Rachel tried to feel as lighthearted as Lily looked. But it was hard. With every improvement Rachel made to Lily's existence, her own seemed to get more complicated.

Chapter Eighteen

The next day, Rachel woke up early after a restless sleep. All night, she'd gone back and forth between nightmares about zombies and anxiety dreams about making all those *Thriller* costumes.

At least I'll have no problem coming up with ideas for the scary costumes, Rachel thought as she stretched and yawned. *I have plenty of inspiration. In fact . . .*

She took a notebook and pencil from her nightstand and began sketching zombies.

There were no glowing hearts or gaping wounds in Rachel's drawings. Now that she'd encountered the actual undead, she knew that high-tech tricks weren't necessary. The *truly* terrifying thing about zombies was the glimmer of life that lingered in their bodies. Rachel wanted to capture that tragic essence in her costumes. She became so immersed in her work that she barely got out of bed until her mom peeked into her room.

"Well, here we go," Dr. Harkness said with a sigh. "You're sleeping in till eleven. You're officially becoming a teenager."

"Sleeping?!" Rachel squawked. "Mom, I've been working since seven!"

"Oh, right," her mom said. She walked in, perched on the edge of Rachel's bed, and squinted at her sketchbook. "The *Thriller* costumes, right?"

"Uh-huh. What do you think of this one?" Rachel asked, pointing at one illustration. It showed a girl in a flowing maxidress with tangles of knotted thread at the wrists, neck, and hem. "I'm calling it corpse chic."

"I think if anyone can make a corpse look stylish, it's you, honey," Rachel's mom said, gazing at the drawing with a mixture of admiration and horror.

"Does that mean you'll drive me to the fabric store in town?" Rachel said. "I need at least a bolt of muslin and lots of other supplies. Too many to carry on my bike."

"Don't you want to take a little time off?" her mom asked. "It *is* Saturday and you look like you could use some fun. You're pale."

Just as she said it, Rachel's stomach growled loudly.

"Rachel!" her mom scolded her. "Have you even eaten? Come downstairs and let me make something for you."

Rachel's thoughts shifted to her *other* job — collecting food for Lily's family.

"Okay," Rachel said, bouncing off her bed. "I'll take some eggs and bacon and some melon? Oh, and how about a side of waffles. Sausage would be good, too."

"All that food?" Rachel's mom responded with a laugh. "Where will you put it?"

"Trust me," Rachel said with an eye roll. "I'll have no problem packing it away."

By the time Lily was due to arrive at Rachel's house, Rachel felt like a superhero.

After she'd eaten a fraction of her groaning brunch, she'd swept the leftovers — along with the contents of the family's new compost container — into a plastic bag. Then she'd surreptitiously hidden it in a sunny, backyard spot to spoil.

She'd also gotten a good start on four costumes and actually finished one of them — Lily's. It was a long gown made of "dirty" rags. Instead of sewing the rags together, Rachel had tied them in knots that made a pretty pattern.

As soon as Lily arrived, Rachel brought her up to her room to show her the dress.

"You like it?" she asked Lily. "It's my homage to your first-day-of-school outfit."

"If you say so," Lily said. She shoved a pile of sewing stuff off the bed so she could carve out a place for herself to sit. Over the course of the day, Rachel's room had started to resemble a tailor's shop. There was hardly any surface that wasn't covered with sketches, spools of thread, and fabric. "I don't think I remember much from that day."

"You did remember about the corn maze today, though," Rachel noted encouragingly. "You even dressed for it."

Lily was wearing her pink tank top and black tutu. Even though the outfit was starting to look seriously bedraggled after living in the demolished barn, it was still more festive than Lily's usual togs.

It also seemed more festive than Lily herself.

Slumped on the edge of Rachel's bed, she stared into space, looking utterly blank.

"Are you *sure* you want to go to the corn maze?" Rachel asked. "What do you think about watching TV instead? Popcorn for me, moldy fruit for you. It'll be fun."

"If you want," Lily said with a shrug. "I only agreed to go because that girl —"

"Megan?" Rachel prompted.

"Megan," Lily said. "She said everybody goes to the corn maze. She said it was . . . classic? I don't know what that means."

"Classic," Rachel explained after pondering it for a moment, "is the kind of fun that people have been having for years and years. Like ice-skating on a frozen pond and drinking cocoa afterward, or going to the drive-in movie theater or drinking one milk shake out of two straws. That kind of thing."

They were the kinds of things, Rachel realized, that Lily had never been able to do. Her parents couldn't take her ice-skating or make her cocoa. As for the drive-in, Lily and her parents were the *subjects* of the kind of horror movies shown there.

Going to the corn maze on a crisp, autumn evening in Iowa *was* classic. And it was something that

Rachel — dreaming of New York — had always taken for granted.

"You know," Rachel told Lily, "Megan's right. Let's go to the corn maze. I kind of think it would be good for both of us."

"Okay," Lily said. She unfurled herself from the bed and headed for the hallway with a spring in her step (or at least a speedy shuffle).

"Wait," Rachel said before Lily reached the door. "You should wear a jacket. And some tights. The temperature's really dropping. Weren't you cold coming over here?"

Lily turned and gave Rachel a baleful look.

"Oh, right," Rachel remembered with a cringe. "I forgot. Zombies — always cold. But you should still wear warm clothes, if only so people won't think, you know . . ."

"*That* I do know," Lily said.

She held up her hand with her fingers outstretched. Her *four* fingers, that was. The gap where her index finger had been looked oozy.

"This might clue people in, too," she said.

"Oh my gosh!" Rachel gasped. "I completely forgot about your finger."

Lily held out her other hand. Sitting on her palm

was her finger, looking pale and shriveled and not very fingerlike. Rachel took a queasy gulp.

"Okay," she said. She began rifling through her basket. "I just need the right shade of thread. Kind of a bluish, grayish, greenish cream."

"Is there a color called Pallor of the Undead?" Lily said. "That would be perfect."

Rachel guffawed, then hurried across the room to shut her bedroom door.

"I just want to make sure nobody in my family peeks in," she explained to Lily. "I think this qualifies as the strangest Saturday night primping *ever*."

It turned out that reattaching a finger was even harder than sewing on an arm. It required tiny, even stitches. By the time Rachel finished, it was four o' clock.

"We better hurry," Rachel said, running to the closet to gather jackets. "I don't want to be in the maze after dusk. It might be classic, but it'll also be creepy."

"Mmmmm," Lily said.

"Oh!" Rachel said. "And you need food. No worries, we can eat on the way."

The girls headed to the maze, about a mile from Rachel's house. As they walked, Lily dipped into the bag of leftovers Rachel had saved for her. The food wasn't quite as disgusting as Lily preferred, but she choked down enough that she could speak again.

And then they arrived at the MacEvoys' farm, home of the corn maze. Rachel watched Lily take it all in. Clusters of little kids ran through the meadow next to the maze. They whooped and laughed and waved candy apples over their heads.

The air smelled like pumpkins, apple cider, and Mrs. MacEvoy's famous sugar-cinnamon cake doughnuts.

People spilled out of the maze exit, laughing and hugging. They pumped their fists in the air and yelled, "We made it!"

"This is classic," Lily said with a big, brown-toothed grin.

"Exactly," Rachel agreed. "I'm so glad we came."

Chapter Nineteen

Twenty minutes after entering the corn maze, Rachel shook her fist at yet another dead end.

"I'm *so* not glad we came," she groaned as she and Lily doubled back. They followed the maze in a different direction, but that route led them to a dead end, too.

"Argh!" Rachel said. "I'm always hopeless in the corn maze. I seriously should have dropped bread crumbs along the way."

"Yeah," Lily agreed, "so I could eat them."

She wrapped her arms around her skinny midsection.

"You're hungry?" Rachel asked with a hint of annoyance in her voice. "A*gain?*"

"We haven't exactly been walking around this

maze at a leisurely pace," Lily complained. "We've practically been jogging."

"Because the sun's setting," Rachel said, glancing at the darkening sky. She dug into the purse she'd brought along.

"Let's see," she murmured. "Oh, look, here's half a packet of pretzels I forgot about. Bonus — they're totally stale."

Lily snatched the cellophane bag from Rachel and devoured the no-longer-crunchy pretzels.

"Mmmm," she moaned, almost as if the pretzels had made her more hungry instead of less.

Desperately, Rachel plunged her hand into the bottom of her purse.

"Ooh," she said, pulling out a round, orange candy. "How about an M&M? It's peanut!"

"Mmmm." Lily reached for the M&M, but instead of taking it, she batted it out of Rachel's hand.

"Lily!" Rachel said, rubbing her smarting hand. Now her annoyance was turning to anger. "It's not like *you've* been any help getting us out of here."

"MMMMMMM!" Lily growled.

"Okay," Rachel breathed in a shaky voice. "Lily, just calm down."

Lily stomped slowly toward Rachel.

"MMMMMM!"

She flailed her hand out again, this time hitting Rachel's arm.

"Ow!"

Lily didn't acknowledge that she'd hurt Rachel. She just took one more shuffling step toward her.

Then another.

And another.

She bent down toward Rachel, huffing at her with breath that smelled like sunbaked garbage.

"MMMMMMMM!"

Lily threw both arms above her head, ready to pounce on Rachel.

"Lily, no!" Rachel shrieked. She ducked just in time to evade Lily's attack and ran!

"Mmmm, mmmmm, mmmm!"

Rachel could hear Lily huffing and puffing several lengths behind her as she scrambled around corners and through corridors, desperately searching for the exit.

To make matters worse, after turning one corner, Rachel saw that the way was blocked by a cluster of high school kids — three boys and three girls, all of them flirting and giggling as they debated whether to go right or left.

"'Scuse me!" Rachel shrieked as she approached them. "Can we get through? It's an emergency!"

One of the girls grimaced at Rachel sympathetically.

"Oh," she said, looking over Rachel's shoulder at Lily. "Your friend is claustrophobic, isn't she? I've seen this happen a million times. Is she totally freaking out?"

Rachel looked at Lily's clumsily flailing limbs, her matted hair, and her murderous black eyes.

"Um, yeah, that's it," she said. "Plus, she really, really has to go to the bathroom!"

"Middle schoolers!" one of the boys complained. "Such amateurs. Okay, folks, coming through!"

The boy, who had the beefy body and brushy crew cut of a football player, began charging through the maze.

Just as Rachel began to follow him, Lily caught up to her and grabbed a hank of her hair.

"Yeow!" Rachel yelled, jerking her head forward to pull her hair out of Lily's grip. It worked — she freed herself.

I only hope I didn't just rip off her finger again, Rachel thought as she darted after Football Boy. *I worked hard sewing that thing on!*

"Mmmmmm!"

Clearly, Rachel hadn't hurt Lily too badly, because she was still hot on her heels.

"Do you know where you're going?" Rachel yelled as Football Boy ran left, then right, then right again.

"Totally!" he called over his shoulder. "I've been through this maze six times."

"Mmmmmm!" Lily groaned.

"Wow, she's really gotta go, huh?" Football Boy huffed.

"Like you wouldn't believe," Rachel puffed.

"Well, no worries," he replied, "because we're out!"

Football Boy plunged through the last corridor and exited into the open air.

As she emerged behind him, Rachel gasped with relief — even though Lily was still chasing her. Rachel kept on running.

"Thank yooooooouuuuu!" she yelled to Football Boy as she sprinted past him. She headed for the MacEvoys' chicken barn, praying there'd be some eggs inside.

Just as she hoped, Lily continued to chase her.

"Hey," Football Boy called after them. "You're going the wrong way. The bathrooms are in the other direction!"

Rachel didn't have time to explain. She was too busy running for her life.

When she reached the barn, she yanked open the door and ran for the nesting box. She knew just where to find it because she used to play there with Megan when they were little. Rachel also knew that if she just kept running, the clucking chickens milling about the barn floor would skitter out of her way.

Luckily, Lily *didn't* know this, and she slowed down, bewildered by the feathered flock in her way. She kicked at the chickens, then slowly began stomping toward Rachel.

"Please let there be eggs, please let there be eggs," Rachel gasped. She started at one end of the long, hay-lined nesting box. Tossing handfuls of the straw over her shoulders, Rachel found . . . nothing. Moving down the box, she found more nothing. She was beginning to panic when her fingers finally found an egg, still warm.

Rachel cringed. This egg couldn't have been any fresher, which meant it was definitely not to Lily's taste.

On the other hand, it was a *raw* egg. Even fresh raw eggs were gooey and gross. So maybe it would work? Rachel had no choice but to try.

"Lily!" Rachel ordered, turning and stalking toward her hungry friend. "Eat this!"

She shoved the egg at Lily's face. Lily bit it into it, shell and all. She chewed madly for a moment, then moaned with pleasure. She gobbled down the rest of the egg, licking the raw, orange yolk from her fingers.

Rachel wanted to hurl, but instead she ran back to the nesting box. She found two more eggs and gave them to Lily, who devoured them as quickly as she had the first.

Within a minute, the crazy had cleared from Lily's eyes. Her moaning had ceased. And, most important, she'd stopped treating Rachel as prey. She became her friend once again.

"See?" she said to Rachel, her voice extra scratchy after all the growling and moaning. "Who says I was no help getting us out of the maze?"

Chapter Twenty

Over the next two weeks, Rachel worked so hard, she started to feel like the walking dead herself.

She started sewing the minute she got home from school each day. She barely broke for dinner, sped through her homework, then sewed some more, often staying bent over her machine until midnight.

Every morning, she went to school early to conduct fittings with *Thriller* cast members. That was her favorite part of the process — nipping, tucking, draping, and devising ways to make each outfit even more fabulous.

And her favorite cast member? That was Jeremy Shay.

She did his fitting in Ms. Greene's classroom. While the teacher sat in the corner taking loud slurps of coffee and applying her sparkly eye makeup, Jeremy stood on a low stool so Rachel could hem his trousers.

They were trousers (as opposed to pants) because Jeremy was supposed to be a Confederate soldier from the Civil War, dead for 150 years before coming back to life to do some Michael Jackson moves. Rachel had torn many holes in the light-colored, high-waisted pants. She'd splashed them with tea and smudged them with potting soil to give them a real died-in look.

"How does that fit?" Rachel asked after she'd finished pinning Jeremy's cuffs. "Can you moonwalk in those?"

He jumped off the stool, did a few sliding steps, and grinned.

"These are perfect," he said. "I feel super undead."

"Ha, ha," Rachel said. She smiled even though Jeremy was clearly teasing her.

"I'm serious," Jeremy said. "Everybody in the cast has been talking about it. Your costumes make us feel like real zombies. It's like you're making us do a better job!"

"You're kidding," Rachel said, feeling light-headed suddenly. "You haven't *really* been saying that, have you?"

"We totally have," Jeremy insisted. "Ask Luke and Olivia. They were both there. Olivia said she loves her shredded dress so much, she's going to ask you to make her a real one. You know, without the blood spatters on it."

"Wow," Rachel breathed. Suddenly, she felt she had to sit down.

"Are you okay?" Jeremy said, pushing his stool toward Rachel so she could lower herself onto it. "You look a little tired."

"Um, I was too rushed to eat breakfast this morning," Rachel admitted. "Plus, what you just told me made me insanely happy. It gives me hope that I could maybe be an actual fashion designer one day."

"*Could* be?" Jeremy said. He pointed at a nearby clothes rack. It was stuffed with dirty, shredded, yet somehow chic *Thriller* costumes. "Rachel, you already *are* one."

"I agree," Ms. Greene piped up from her corner. "If you're not careful, I'm going to have you do *all* the costumes for next year's revue."

"Wow," Rachel whispered. "Wow, wow, wow."

Of course, that's when the bell rang, bringing her back to earth, back to her sore neck, burning eyes, and fingers dotted with needle pricks.

Rachel's hands weren't just scabby with sewing injuries. They also smelled faintly of rotten food. After the Great Corn Maze Almost-Massacre, she'd been stashing as much food as she could. She made sure Lily had regular snacks through the school day, then always tried to send her home with a huge load of spoils from the Dumpster.

It seemed to be enough. Lily acted normal (well, normal for Lily) throughout the day. Her parents seemed satisfied, too. They were still hiding in their barn, and the people of Slayton were still blissfully ignorant of their zombie neighbors.

That didn't stop Rachel from worrying. She'd learned from the corn maze that high-stress situations and exercise *really* brought out the zombie in Lily.

And what's more stressful and calorie-burning than singing and dancing in front of a huge audience? Rachel thought grimly.

So, as the revue drew ever closer, Rachel stepped up her food gathering. She carved out so many hiding places for her rotten food, she started to feel like a dog burying bones and forgetting where half of them were. At the same time, she started staying up later and later to get all the costumes finished in time.

By the time show day arrived, Rachel was ready to collapse. But she couldn't. If she was going to protect all of Slayton from a zombified Lily, she needed to be completely on her game.

Ms. Greene had ordered all members of the revue cast to show up at the high school auditorium two hours before the seven o'clock show.

So Rachel told Lily to come to her house at four for a heavy meal of gluey, old oatmeal and petrified sausage links.

It worked. When the girls arrived at the auditorium, Lily was full of energy (for Lily, anyway). She was wearing her knotty nightgown and a pair of high-ankled boots. Her hair was arranged in a thick braid. Rachel had persuaded Lily to forgo her usual rainbow of hair extensions because it didn't fit her character.

"But I'll put a stash of them in my hair," Rachel had promised, clipping a bunch into her locks. "And I'll give some to you after the show.

"More importantly," Rachel had told Lily, "I'm packing a bag of food for you. I'll remind you to eat something every half hour. That way, you won't . . . you know . . ."

"Try to eat some*one*," Lily finished for her. "I know. Don't worry, Rachel. You've planned for everything. The revue's going to be great."

Clearly, Lily didn't know this law of the theater world: *Never* say the show's going to be great. If you do, something will surely go wrong.

In Rachel's case, it was *three* things that went wrong.

It started backstage with Olivia's "blood"-spattered dress. As Rachel was helping Jeremy gel his hair into scary-looking spikes, Olivia tapped her on the shoulder.

"Look," she said.

Rachel glanced at the dress, then gasped. The bright red ink — which Olivia was supposed to dramatically reveal halfway through the song by ripping off her coat — had somehow turned purple! Purple wasn't scary! Purple was silly! The big reveal was going to be ruined!

"How did that happen?" Rachel exclaimed.

"I have no idea!" Olivia said. "Maybe I shouldn't

have hung the costume in front of the window, especially since we've had so much sunshine the past few days?"

"*May*be," Rachel said, frowning at Olivia. A moment later, though, she snapped her fingers. "Red lipstick! There's got to be one lying around here somewhere. Olivia, go find it. I'll just trace over the purple blood. You don't even have to take your costume off."

While Rachel was smearing lipstick onto Olivia, she felt another tap on her shoulder.

This time, it was Luke. He was dressed as a Union soldier to counter Jeremy's Confederate one. Except there was no way he was equipped to fight — or sing and dance, for that matter. His pants were falling down!

"Do you have a belt or something to hold these up?" Luke asked Rachel.

"Um, *no*," Rachel said. "I didn't sew belt loops on your trousers because I measured them to fit you exactly. And I put four buttons on, which are totally accurate for the Civil War period."

"Except that they're missing," Olivia noted, pointing at Luke's buttonless pants.

Luke looked guilty.

"I was trying to bulk up for wrestling tryouts," he admitted.

"Bulk up?" Rachel said. "With what, weights?"

"Ice cream," Luke corrected her. He showed her the ice cream belly he'd developed in the two weeks since Rachel had fitted him with his soldier's uniform. "The buttons kind of popped off."

"Okay, okay," Rachel said, feeling frazzled. "I'll sew more buttons on. Go change."

As she finished Olivia's lipstick and started Luke's buttons, she scanned the backstage area. It was crowded with Beatles, folk singers, a young Elvis, and an old Elvis, but no very tall zombies.

"Has anyone seen Lily?" she asked. "It's six o'clock."

"What's important about six o'clock?" Megan asked, perching in front of Rachel's chair. "I mean, besides dinner. I just came over to see if you wanted some."

"Dinner?" Rachel said.

"Yeah, don't you smell it?" Megan said. She pointed to a folding table on the other side of the backstage area. It was piled high with pizza boxes. Now that Megan mentioned it, Rachel realized that the pizza did smell incredible.

"Ms. Greene ordered in for the whole cast!" Megan said happily. "Oh, and speaking of Lily, I did see her over there."

"Really?" Rachel said.

"Yeah, it was weird," Megan said. She paused to laugh as three girls dressed like the Supremes started doing the Pony. Then she finished what she was saying.

"Lily took one whiff of the pizza and practically ran away," she said. "Maybe she doesn't like extra cheese?"

"Definitely not," Rachel said, just as the Supremes broke into song. "She's lactose intolerant, just like all zom —"

Rachel gulped back the second half of the word and froze.

"Like all what?" Megan shouted. "I can't hear you over the Supremes!"

"Oh, nothing!" Rachel said, sighing with relief. That had been close! She popped out of her chair. "Anyway, I'll go find Lily. Maybe she'll prefer pepperoni."

"Aren't you going to finish my pants first?" Luke complained. He was sitting in a chair nearby, wearing a pair of shiny basketball shorts.

Rachel plunked herself back into her chair and took up her needle and thread.

"Five minutes," she muttered to herself. "That's all I need. Then I'll go find Li —"

"Rachel, darling."

Rachel froze and twisted in her chair to see Ms. Greene holding the gothic governess costume that Rachel had made for Lacey Davison, another cast member.

"Here's the bad news," Ms. Greene said, "Lacey came down with a sudden stomach bug an hour ago."

"And the good news?" Rachel quavered.

"She managed not to get any vomit on her costume!" Ms. Greene announced. "But of course, she's out of the show."

Rachel groaned.

"Ah, but I have another bit of good news," Ms. Greene said. She thrust the costume toward Rachel. "You and Lacey are almost exactly the same size."

"What?" Rachel squeaked. "What do you mean?"

"I mean you're taking her place in the act," Ms. Greene announced, with a big, lipsticky smile. "Welcome to showbiz, darling."

Chapter Twenty-One

During the next forty-five minutes, Rachel piled her hair into an off-kilter pompadour, then sprayed it black. On a whim, she decided to add her hair extensions to her updo. She thought the rainbow of stripes would add some unexpected modern flavor to her outfit.

She made up her face with white makeup and black eyeliner. She zipped herself into Lacey's cobwebby dress, noting how the skirt swung prettily around her legs and the wrist-length sleeves elongated her arms. Then Rachel bounced like a pinball from one *Thriller* cast member to the next as they taught her the moves for their big dance number.

She kept trying to slip away to talk to Lily, whom she saw lurking along the sidelines. But every time she did, someone else cornered her, saying, "Okay, here's the part where Lacey pretends to break a tombstone over her head," or "Let's see if your moon-walk is up to par."

Before Rachel knew it, the first act — young Elvis and a bevy of backup singers — was taking the stage! Everyone else crowded into the wings to watch the performers and peek through the curtain at the audience.

While they watched, Rachel resumed her search for Lily. She pushed her way through Beatles, Supremes, and folksingers, hissing, "Lily? Where are you?"

She grabbed zombie after zombie only to realize each one was a *Thriller* performer and not the *real* zombie she was looking for. But finally, Rachel tracked Lily down. She was clinging to a stage cur-tain as though she didn't have the strength to stand on her own. She looked so pale that Rachel won-dered if she'd caked white makeup on top of her already ghostly skin.

Then she saw that Lily's mouth was dry and her fingers were shaking with hunger. That was no stage makeup. Lily needed nourishment immediately!

"Lily!" Rachel whispered urgently. "Where's that bag of food I packed for you?"

Lily frowned as she tried to remember. Then she shook her head and shrugged.

"This is *bad*," Rachel said, wringing her hands.

"Mmmm," Lily groaned.

"Scratch that, this is *really* bad," Rachel said. She took Lily's clammy hand and pulled her away from the other kids. On the folding table against the wall, she spotted a couple of open pizza boxes left from the dinner Ms. Greene had brought in.

"Do you think you can choke down some pizza?" Rachel asked Lily. "I'm sure it's nice and cold and gross now. We can peel off the cheese."

"Mmmmm," Lily said.

"I'm going to take that as a yes," Rachel said. She flipped open a pizza box and found a cold, stiff piece of crust.

"Here," Rachel said, giving it to Lily. "Chow down. I think we go on in about ten minutes and I've *got* to practice this dance routine one more time."

While Lily gnawed on the pizza crust, Rachel hummed the tune to *Thriller* and ran through the routine's side-to-side head bobble and clawlike hand motions. She rehearsed the dance two full times, then turned to smile at Lily.

"What do you think?" she said. "Have I got it?"

"Mmmmm," Lily moaned.

"Oh, no," Rachel said. "Is the food not helping?"

Lily held up the cold, tough pizza crust with one hand. In the other, she cupped a small, brownish pebble.

"What is that?" Rachel asked. She leaned in to take a closer look at the little rock in Lily's palm. Then she gasped and jumped backward.

"Lily, is that a tooth?" she whispered. "*Your* tooth?"

"Pizza crust," Lily grunted. "Pulled it out. Mmmmm."

"Okay, *that's* not good," Rachel said.

"*Thriller* cast!" Ms. Greene whisper-shouted to the group. "Two minutes!"

Rachel stood on her tiptoes and tried to meet Lily's vacant-looking, black eyes.

"Can you hold it together until after our number?" Rachel asked her. "Then, I promise we'll find you something better to eat."

"Mmmmm," Lily answered.

Rachel wanted to grab Lily by the shoulders and shake some life back into her. But she worried that doing it would only make something else fall off Lily's decaying body. So instead, she snapped her fingers in front of Lily's eyes.

"Lily!" she hissed. "Are you there? Are you okay?"

Lily shook her head and blinked several times. Then her eyes defogged and she seemed to come back to herself.

"Okay," she said. "I can do this."

She even did a little head bobble from the *Thriller* dance to prove it.

"Yes!" Rachel said. "Lily, you're awesome! Let's go."

The two girls joined the rest of the "zombies" in the wings on either side of the stage. Rachel had only a few seconds to take in all her handiwork: Jeremy and Luke in their soldier uniforms, Olivia in her blood-spattered shreds, Megan looking very bride-of-Frankenstein in a dirt-smeared white dress, and of course, Lily in her high-fashion-meets-graveyard knotted gown.

Rachel had never felt so proud. Not only had she created all these costumes, she'd done it for a bevy of different bodies. Olivia was short and curvy, basically the complete opposite of Lily's tall, skinny fashion model self. Yet she looked gorgeous and glamorous in her bloody frock. So did Megan, who was usually the first to admit that she was all big feet and knobby knees. Tonight, though, she looked like a graceful, gruesome pixie in the long-skirted gown that Rachel had made for her.

As for her own costume, Rachel felt relieved to wear something that embraced her solid, sporty figure after always trying to cram herself into long, lean, runway-ready looks. As a result, she had to admit that she looked pretty fabulous.

Knowing she'd handmade every last one of these costumes filled Rachel with such a surge, she forgot to feel nervous about performing with hardly any preparation.

She forgot that the audience was packed with people, including her parents.

She forgot that Lily had just come dangerously close to going full-on zombie.

All she felt was energy and excitement. When she and the fourteen other performers took the stage and began to pull out their Michael Jackson moves, it was clear Rachel wasn't the only one. They were killing it (so to speak). Their dance moves were crisp and coordinated, their singing was in sync and high volume, and they couldn't have looked more creepy or cool.

Is it really true what Jeremy said? Rachel wondered as she followed the group into the big finale. *Are they inspired by my costumes?*

There was no way to know for sure. But there was no question about what the audience thought of *Thriller.* As soon as the performers froze in a final chilling pose, the auditorium erupted. There was applause and stomps and hoots and even tossed flowers. One of them bonked Rachel in the head. She put her hand over her eyes to see who had thrown it and saw her parents waving at her from the front row.

Then — after Ms. Greene had shooed them back to a hallway behind the stage so the next act could go on — all the performers began jumping and hugging.

"We *rocked*!" Luke said, grinning through his ghoulish makeup.

"I love you guys so much," Olivia shrieked, hugging everyone she could.

Jeremy bounced around the hallway, high-fiving his friends. But when he landed before Rachel, he stared at her, his smile fading into something more serious.

Then he bent down and wrapped her in a big hug. He smelled really good, like a combination of corn silk, soap, and pizza crust. It took Rachel's breath away. When the hug ended, she expected Jeremy to continue on his high-fiving way. But he just stood there, grinning at Rachel. It felt like they could have stayed in that spot, smiling at each other forever.

Who knew, maybe they would have — if they hadn't been interrupted.

By Lily.

She appeared, as if out of nowhere, looming over Jeremy. Her hair was wilder than ever. Her eyes were blank and bottomless. Her lips were bared, revealing a mouth full of pointy, brown teeth (and one bloody gap).

With a roar, she sank those teeth into Jeremy's shoulder!

Chapter Twenty-Two

"Noooooo!" Rachel screamed.

She leaped toward Lily and tried to push her away from Jeremy, but when she did, she heard a sickening tearing sound. It was the sound, Rachel knew, of Jeremy's skin and muscle coming away in Lily's mouth. It was the sound of Lily's zombie virus entering Jeremy's bloodstream, consigning him to an endless existence of decay and deterioration, of being ostracized by society, of constantly lusting for human blood and guts.

Jeremy would now begin the nonlife of a zombie. It would last, horribly, forever.

And it was all Rachel's fault.

Rachel squeezed her eyes shut, bracing herself for Jeremy's screams of pain and horror.

But . . . they never came.

Rachel popped her eyes open to see Jeremy gaping at the shoulder of his costume. Layers of wool, shoulder pad, and shirt had been torn away, but his skin was perfectly intact!

Lily, meanwhile, was spitting out a mouthful of fabric and cotton batting.

"Lily?!" Jeremy said. "What the heck?"

Lily looked up at him and growled — before she pounced again!

But this time, Rachel was ready! She jumped in front of Jeremy.

"No, Lily!" she grunted as she pushed at her lunging, flailing friend. "I can't let you turn Jeremy into a zombie!"

"A *what*?!" Jeremy yelled. "Rachel, what are you talking about?"

With that, everyone in the hallway stopped hooting and hugging. In fact, they went eerily silent. The only sound in the place was Lily moaning and growling and Rachel huffing and puffing as she tried to fight her off.

"I'll . . . explain . . . everything . . ." Rachel grunted. "But first . . . a little *help*?"

"Oh yeah, sorry!" Jeremy said. He jumped in to help Rachel fight Lily off. Lily flailed and scratched at them until Megan and Luke snuck up behind her and grabbed her arms. Each took one of Lily's hands and held them behind her back.

With Lily captured, everyone stared at Rachel through their gray-shadowed makeup, waiting for an explanation.

"It's true," Rachel announced to them. "Lily's a zombie. But she and I have got it under control, I promise."

"Hello?" Olivia burst out, pointing at Lily with a black-painted fingernail. "She just tried to *eat* your boyfriend. That doesn't seem 'under control' to me!"

"Boyfriend?!" Rachel squeaked. She glanced at Jeremy and blushed. "What do you mean, boyfriend?"

"Listen, don't take this the wrong way," Jeremy said, grunting as he continued to fend off Lily, "but can we talk about that *later*?"

"Oh, right, right," Rachel said. "Of course."

Then she addressed her friends.

"Listen, you guys, yes, Lily is a zombie, but she's also a good person, or whatever. She really doesn't want to hurt anybody."

"Could have fooled me," Olivia said, glowering at Lily.

"Mmmmmmm!" Lily growled back.

"This is only because she's desperately hungry," Rachel said. "If I just make sure she eats enough rotten fruits and veggies and spoiled meat and stuff like that, she's *fine*."

"Until," Jeremy pointed out, glancing at the rip in his costume, "she's not."

Rachel felt tears well up in her eyes. She sniffled and looked at the floor.

"You're right," she whispered. "I was an idiot to think I could handle a whole family of zombies on my own."

"Wait, a *family*?" Luke shouted from behind Lily.

"Oh, yeah," Rachel said, looking up at him. "Lily's parents are zombies, too. Did I not mention that?"

"No, you sort of forgot that part!" Olivia said with a glare.

Rachel burst into tears.

"I'm *so* sorry, you guys," she said.

"Rachel . . ." Jeremy's voice was soft and sweet and understanding. Before Rachel knew it, his arms were wrapped around her again. It turned out a consoling hug from Jeremy? It felt every bit as nice as a celebratory one.

At least, it did for a split second. Then Megan shouted, "Jeremy, why'd you let go of Lily? I can't hold on!"

Rachel and Jeremy looked up in time to see Lily wrench her right arm out of Megan's grip.

Now the only one who had Lily was Luke. He was valiantly clinging to her left arm.

"You can't get away, zombie!" he shouted. Then to Rachel, he said, "See? I told you I was bulking up!"

"Yay, Luke!" Olivia shouted. A bunch of other kids cheered along with her. "You've got her!"

And he did — until Lily lunged for Luke's face with her teeth!

"Luke, watch out!" Rachel shrieked. "If she bites you, you'll become a zombie, too!"

"Whoa!" Luke cried. He let go of Lily's arm and leaped backward.

With that, Lily was loose. She spun around, sizing up all the kids who surrounded her. She growled and scowled, but she didn't seem ready to make a move.

"Hey," Rachel whispered to Jeremy. "I just thought of something. We *all* look just like Lily, like zombies!

Maybe she's far gone enough that she's forgotten who we are. Maybe she won't attack people she thinks are her own kind."

"Maybe," Jeremy replied hopefully.

Suddenly, Lily crouched to the floor, arching her back like a cat about to pounce.

And then, that's just what she did!

"MMMMMMM!" she roared. She leaped toward the closest kid, a sixth grader named Henry Schultz.

"Or maybe not," Jeremy shouted. "Everybody, *run!*"

Jeremy pulled Rachel by one hand and Henry by the other. He began racing them toward an exit door at the end of the hallway. With all the other *Thriller* performers crowded behind them, they burst out the door into a parking lot behind the high school. Then they scattered.

Henry broke away from Jeremy and ran with a pack of other sixth graders around the school. Another bunch of kids charged around the school in the other direction.

Jeremy, Rachel, Olivia, and Luke ran straight, away from the school and toward a corn farm that lay beyond it.

It was they who Lily followed.

She lumbered after them. She was as clumsy as always, but with her long legs and her monstrous appetite, she was definitely still a threat.

"Let's go to the barn and hide in there!" Rachel huffed, pointing at the big red barn to the right of the cornfield. A light glowed inside.

"If we shut the doors," Rachel told her friends, "that should keep Lily out. Zombies don't do well against obstacles."

The group sprinted to the barn and plunged inside while Jeremy and Luke each grasped one of the big, sliding doors. They ran toward each other, dragging them closed.

But the huge doors were heavy and slow.

"Aaaah!" Olivia screamed, pointing through the narrowing gap between the doors. Lily had arrived in the dirt clearing in front of the barn and was charging for them.

Rachel leaped to Jeremy's side to help him pull his door closed, while Olivia lent her muscle to Luke's door.

Just before Lily plunged through the doors, the four kids managed to clank them closed.

"*Rawwwwrrr!*" Lily howled from outside the barn. She banged on the doors in a rage.

"This is *really* scary, you guys!" Olivia cried.

"No, we can handle this!" Rachel shouted. She ran to the barn wall and began to pull down tools — a shovel and rake, a mallet, and a coil of rope.

Boom, boom, boom! Lily continued to pound on the doors.

"Everybody," Rachel ordered her friends, "just look for something Lily can eat. Food will bring her out of this zombified state. Look for moldy hay. Rotten eggs. Old chicken feed. Oh, and if you find any dead mice or rats in traps, that would be great!"

"Gross!" Olivia cried. "Rachel, are you serious?"

Boom, boom, boom!

"There's no time to be skeeved out now," Rachel yelled. "You'll get used to Lily's diet, I promise. Now go, go, go!"

The group fanned out to search for zombie food, but before they got very far —

Boom, boom, CRASH!

Lily splintered the heavy barn doors and landed inside the building, her arms outstretched like claws, her mouth open wide and howling!

Chapter Twenty-Three

"I got this!" Luke yelled. Brandishing the shovel that Rachel had pulled from the wall of tools, he charged at Lily.

Unexpectedly, Lily charged right back at him! She jerked the shovel out of his hands and snapped the heavy wooden handle in two!

"Um," Luke huffed, running back to their arsenal of farm tools. "I think I need some backup!"

While he scooped up a mallet, Jeremy picked up the rake, and Rachel grabbed a rope.

The boys swung at Lily with their tools, but Lily blocked their every blow with her two rods of wood. She might have been slow and clumsy, but in her rage, she was also supernaturally strong. There was no touching her.

To Rachel, this was a good thing.

"You guys," she cried to Jeremy and Luke. "Don't hurt Lily. Just try to pin her down so I can tie her up with this rope!"

"Are you kidding?" Luke yelled, mid-battle. "Rachel, she's a zombie! As in brain-eating, gut-chomping undead monster!"

"Yeah, but it's not *her* fault!" Rachel defended Lily. "She was born that way. She didn't ask to be a monster. And anyway, monster or not, I care about her."

Only when Rachel reached the end of her speech did she realize that the *clanging* and *thwacking* of the farm tools had ceased. Lily had stopped fighting off the boys and was staring at Rachel. Her black eyes suddenly seemed less vacant and more human.

Jeremy and Luke looked with uncertainty at the two girls.

"There, there," Rachel said to Lily, the way you would try to soothe a scared animal. "If you stop fighting, we can give you something to eat."

Behind her back, she motioned frantically at Olivia, who'd been cowering behind her. Rachel *really* hoped she'd found something for Lily to eat.

Rachel closed her eyes with relief when Olivia placed something in her hand. It was cold and round and the size of a soccer ball. Rachel had no idea what it was.

"Okay, here you go, Lily," Rachel said, still in the same soothing voice. Slowly, she brought her hand forward and held it out to Lily. Only then did she see what she was offering the zombie.

It was a cabbage. A nice, fresh, pale green, probably-just-picked cabbage.

Lily took one sniff, then roared with renewed rage. She batted the fresh vegetable out of Rachel's hand with such force that it exploded against the barn wall.

Rachel crouched and threw her arms over her head, certain that Lily was going to attack her. But instead, her friend turned and ran, howling, out of the barn. She plunged into the cornfield just beyond the clearing and disappeared from view.

Rachel jumped to her feet and whirled to glare at Olivia.

"A *fresh* cabbage?!" she shrieked. *"Olivia!"*

"I'm sorry, it was all I could find," Olivia said, pointing at a pickup truck parked in the barn. Its bed was brimming with veggies that the barn's owner must have just picked for that weekend's farmers' market.

"You couldn't find *one* dead mouse?" Rachel complained.

"You guys, shhhhh!" Jeremy hissed. He ran out into the clearing, cocked his head, and pointed into the cornfield. His friends joined him outside and followed his gaze.

Unlike Jeremy's mom's sweet corn, which was harvested during the summer, this field was full of field corn. Field corn stalks weren't harvested until the late fall, when the corn was dry and crunchy. So these plants were about ten feet tall and they hid Lily completely.

But if the group couldn't see Lily in the field, they could hear her. Her breathing was raspy and ragged. Her shuffling feet rustled in the dirt.

As Rachel's eyes adjusted to the darkness, she also realized she *could* tell where Lily was — by watching the tops of the cornstalks moving.

Lily was plowing straight down one of the rows — and she was headed back to the high school. Hundreds of people, including Rachel's parents, were probably streaming out of the building now.

Make that hundreds of potential meals, Rachel thought ominously.

"Guys," she said. "Lily's still hungry. We can't let her get away!"

"Let's get herrrrrrr!" Luke shouted, plunging into the cornfield.

Whooping, Jeremy followed him.

"Aaaannd, there goes our element of surprise," Rachel said, turning to Olivia with an eye roll. "Boys!"

"Yup," Olivia complained. "Now we have no choice but to join the chase. We can't let Lily out of there."

With that, the girls dashed after the boys.

"Lily!" Rachel called. "Please let us catch up to you. I promise, we'll get you something better to eat."

"Much better than all those people at the high school, we swear!" Olivia yelled from nearby.

"Olivia!" shouted Luke and Jeremy together from somewhere else in the field.

"Sorry!"

"Mmmmmm!"

Rachel cocked an ear. Lily's distinctive moan had come from somewhere to her left.

"You guys," Rachel called out. "That's her. Everybody go left!"

They turned and began crashing through the corn. For a moment, all Rachel could hear was huffing and puffing and the occasional "Ow!" when someone got thwacked by a stiff stalk.

But a moment later, she heard Jeremy yell, "Gotcha!"

"Jeremy!" Olivia's voice shrieked. "I'm not Lily. I'm Olivia!"

"Oh, sorry!" Jeremy said. "In your zombie outfit, you look just like her!"

Rachel shook her head in frustration and overtook them.

"We've got to get Lily!" she yelled — just before *she* crashed into somebody!

Somebody who grabbed her and held on tight.

"Scratch that!" Rachel screamed into the darkness. "Lily's got me!"

"Wait, what?" her captor said.

"Luke?" Rachel said.

"Rachel?" Luke replied.

Rachel yelled to the others, "Never mind. Another case of mistaken identity."

"You know," Luke complained, "you really did *too* good a job on these zombie costumes."

A moment later, Jeremy and Olivia caught up to them.

"We can't find her!" Jeremy said breathlessly.

"What are going to do?" Olivia cried, on the verge of tears. "Does anyone have a cell phone? Maybe we should we call the police?"

"No!" Rachel cried. "If we do that, Lily might really get hurt."

"I hate to say it, Rachel," Jeremy said, "but that might be necessary to stop her."

"No!" Rachel cried again, feeling tears spring to her own eyes. "I won't let that happen."

"Well, what do you think we should do?"

"I don't knooooow," Rachel groaned. She raked her fingers through her hair, pulling out a tangled handful of hair extensions as she did.

Rachel stared at the rainbow of fake hair in her hand, then gasped.

"Wait a minute!" she said. "I *do* know what to do. But we have to get to the far end of the field before Lily does. Everybody out! We'll run around the outside of the field and intercept her there!"

Chapter Twenty-Four

Rachel began sprinting back toward the barn with her friends on her heels. When she burst out of the cornstalks into the dirt clearing, she made a sharp right and began to run along the perimeter of the field. At the exact point that Lily would emerge if she was going to take the shortest route back to the school, Rachel began draping her hair extensions on various corn plants. They glinted in the moonlight and fluttered in the chilly, autumn breeze.

"I hope this works," she muttered.

She motioned to her friends to hide in some cornstalks a short distance away. Then she whispered to Luke, "Sneak back to the barn and get that rope."

While he did, the rest of them waited.

Rachel could feel her heart pounding. Every second seemed to crawl by. But before she knew it, she heard Lily's telltale foot-shuffling and raspy breathing.

She broke free of the cornstalks! She looked around.

Please see the hair extensions, Rachel begged her silently. *You know you love them!*

Lily began to lumber toward the high school.

Olivia started to gasp, but Rachel slapped her hand over her friend's mouth. There was still a chance.

Lily cocked her head and turned to look in their direction. Now she began lumbering toward *them.*

Oh, no! Rachel screamed inside her head. *She heard Olivia. We're goners.*

But just before she got close enough to spot them, something seemed to catch Lily's eye. Something curly and hot pink and fluttering from an ear of corn.

Lily turned and lurched toward the hair extensions. One by one, she began to pluck the shiny strands of hair from the cornstalks and poke them into her own matted mane.

She was so absorbed in these little bits of beauty

that she didn't hear Luke tiptoeing up behind her and —

"You're going down, Lily!" he shouted. He pounced on her, making her drop all her hair extensions. "For real, this time!"

The rest of the kids rushed out to help him, and within a minute, Lily's hands were tied behind her back. Growling, she squirmed and fought the rope.

"I'm sorry, Lily," Rachel said, her voice choked up. "But we have no choice."

"Mmmmmmm!" Lily said. And then — she ripped her own shoulder out of its socket! She tore the stitches Rachel had made and let her arm dangle from the ropes binding her wrists. This loosened the rope enough to set her other arm free.

"Aaaaaigggh!" screamed Rachel and her friends.

They got ready to run — but to their shock, Lily didn't try to capture them, or scratch them, or bite them. She didn't seem interested in them at all.

All she wanted to do was crouch to the ground to collect the fallen hair extensions. She picked them up and tried to go back to clipping them into her hair.

But with only one arm to work with, and her fingers shaking with hunger, Lily kept dropping the bright bundles in the dirt. She growled, scrabbled for the hair extensions, and tried once more, only to drop them again. Rachel braced herself. Would Lily's frustration drive her to attack again?

Surprisingly, no. She didn't pounce on her friends with murderous rage. And she didn't run away. What she did was drop to her knees and start crying, her muddy tears falling into the dirt beneath her.

Even though Rachel knew Lily was still dangerous, she crouched down next to her and put her hand on the zombie's bony back.

"It's going to be okay," she whispered.

But the fact was, Rachel didn't know if it would be okay. Lily couldn't be trusted. She couldn't maintain friendships. She couldn't even have a little fun wearing kooky extensions in her hair.

She was a zombie and she always would be. She was trapped.

That must have been why Lily barely seemed to notice when Jeremy's father, Sheriff Shay, showed up in his squad car and took her to the Slayton County Jail.

*   *   *

After Sheriff Shay locked Lily in a jail cell, Rachel told him where to find Mr. and Mrs. Hack. Within an hour, they were locked up with their daughter.

The cell was a typical small-town jail, tucked into a corner of the police officers' open office. So Rachel was able to stay there, sitting on a bench just a few feet away from the cell's iron bars.

Once Sheriff Shay had the Hacks all squared away, he called Rachel's parents to come to the station. While she waited for them, Jeremy and the others went out to find the zombie family some food from a nearby Dumpster.

By the time Rachel's parents arrived, looking pale and shaken, the Hacks had eaten and calmed down. Mr. and Mrs. Hack sat on the floor, alternately moaning and staring into space. Lily sat on the little cot in the far corner of the jail cell. She gazed into her lap as more muddy tears trailed down her cheeks.

Rachel felt as miserable as Lily looked. She glanced at Jeremy, who'd joined her on her bench after returning with the food.

"What do you think is going to happen?" she asked. She nodded at Sheriff Shay's desk, where he was talking quietly to Rachel's parents. All three

of the adults were shaking their heads in disbelief. "Do you think they're going to make Lily and her
parents leave town?"

"I don't know," Jeremy said with an unhappy
shrug. "Now that they know the Hacks are zombies, they can't exactly sic them on some other
community."

"You have a point," Rachel said. "So what's the
answer? Do they have to stay locked up forever?"

Jeremy sighed.

"Maybe so," he said.

"Well, that's just awful," Rachel declared.

After one more glance at Lily, she jumped to her
feet and stalked over to Sheriff Shay's desk.

"Sheriff," she said. "Can't you let the Hacks go?
As long as Lily stays away from all future corn mazes
and middle school musicals, I'm sure this kind of
thing won't happen again. The Hacks can stay in
their barn, far away from town. They won't bother
anybody from way out there."

The sheriff regarded Rachel skeptically.

"But can you guarantee that, Rachel?" he asked.

"If I have help getting them enough food," Rachel
said, "I *think* I can guarantee it."

"I'll help!" Jeremy said, jumping to his feet and

hurrying over. "And I know there are plenty of other kids at SMS who will, too. We like Lily, even if she's way more weird than we already thought she was."

"I don't know," Rachel's dad said. "It just seems too risky."

"What if Lily drops out of school?" Rachel proposed. She cringed even as she said it. She hated to send Lily into exile, with no place to go, no books to read, nobody to talk to. But wasn't that better than being banished from Slayton altogether?

The only ones who didn't seem troubled by this dilemma were Lily's parents. They only seemed to want more food. Lurching to their feet, they moaned and shuffled toward the jail cell bars, their arms outstretched.

"Mom, Dad!" Lily cried, jumping to her feet. "No! You're making this worse. Sit down, please."

To Rachel's surprise, Lily's parents listened to her. Clumsily, they plunked themselves back onto the floor.

"Do they understand you?" Rachel asked Lily, moving closer to the cell.

"In their own way," Lily replied with a sad smile. "And in their own way, I know they love me. They want me to be happy. I was happy, too, here in Slayton."

That's when the brownish tears started trailing down Lily's cheeks again.

Rachel turned to Jeremy, her own face crumpling. He moved close to give her another hug. But this time, Rachel realized with a wrinkled nose, he did *not* smell good. He smelled like a Dumpster, like rotten food and other garbage and . . .

"Your mother's cornfield!" Rachel said suddenly, her eyes lighting up.

"Um, what?" Jeremy said.

"You smell like your mom's disgusting cornfield," Rachel declared with a big, happy smile. "You totally stink!"

"Okay, *that's* embarrassing," Jeremy said, quickly shedding his offensive jacket.

"No, it's awesome!" Rachel said excitedly.

She ran back to Sheriff Shay's desk and said, "Sheriff, I have an idea. I know where the Hacks can spend their days *and* have all the food they could ever need. The only thing you have to do is promise *never* to replace the combine at your farm."

Chapter Twenty-Five

Rachel ran into homeroom just as the bell rang. She gave her outfit — a sundress with three different-colored crinolines — a last-minute adjustment as she hurried to her desk on the far side of the room. Flopping into her seat, she inhaled the spring-scented breeze that wafted through the open window.

Then she turned to smile at the girl sitting behind her.

"You're late *again*!" Lily said, frowning with disapproval. But she couldn't maintain her glower, and it quickly morphed into a grin. Her teeth (well, technically they were dentures) were so white and shiny, they practically glowed. And, now that Lily had learned to wear ChapStick instead of eating it, her lips were supple and uncracked.

They were still purplish blue, but you can't have everything.

"I'm still not used to *you* being on time every day," Rachel said to Lily.

"Well, the early bird gets the worm," Lily said. "Literally."

"Oh, so you're still working on the Smiths' grub problem?" Rachel asked. The Smiths lived in a farmhouse not too far from the Hacks.

"Uh-huh!" Lily said, smacking her lips with satisfaction. "Their kitchen garden is absolutely infested. My parents are still there, finishing up. For lunch, they're going to the MacEvoys'. They've got inchworms that are just murdering their mulberry trees. Yum!"

"It's funny," Rachel said, "somehow I'm more freaked out by you being so punctual than by the fact that you and your parents eat bugs for a living."

"And rotten cornstalks," Lily added. "And smashed pumpkins. And roadkill."

"And Slayton's never smelled better," Rachel said with a laugh.

"Speaking of bad smells . . ."

That was Jeremy, who was sitting in the next aisle. He'd overheard Rachel and Lily talking and was now reaching into his backpack. He pulled out a tightly tied plastic bag of black bananas.

"My mom found this at the bottom of our fruit bowl this morning," Jeremy said, handing the bag to Lily. "She knows it's your favorite."

"Jeremy," Rachel said, smiling at him. "That's so sweet."

As he grinned back at her, Rachel wondered if was possible that he'd gotten even cuter since the last time she'd seen him.

Another thing that didn't seem possible? That Lily had almost killed Jeremy only six months earlier.

That was before Rachel had come up with the idea of giving Lily and her parents a job clearing the Shays' cornfield. The Shays paid them for their work and let the Hacks keep (or rather *eat*) all the goopy vegetation that they cleared.

When the Hacks had finished feasting off the Shays' field, it was neatly tilled, well fertilized, and ready for the next growing season. Jeremy's mom had been thrilled.

Soon, other Slayton families started hiring the Hacks to help *them*. The MacEvoys had them clear away a mound of rotten pumpkins. The Harknesses asked them to dispose of an opossum that had been flattened by a truck in front of their house. And once it was discovered that the Hacks considered caterpillars, grubs, and other garden pests an especially nutritious delicacy, they began to get more exterminating jobs than they had time for. Well fed and peaceful, they gained the trust of the people of Slayton.

The Slaytonions even pitched in to haul away the Sarners' decrepit barn. After taking up a collection, they built the Hacks a simple cottage on the same bit of land. There, the zombie family was far enough away that people felt safe in the unlikely event of a craving for brains. Yet the Hacks were close enough that they felt like members of the community.

Especially Lily.

With her improved diet and her very own home, Lily was no longer blank-eyed and dusty. She was way less forgetful than she used to be. She even, occasionally, did her homework and got the answers right. And Lily's wardrobe, thanks to Rachel and her busier-than-ever sewing machine, was *fabulous*.

Lily's wasn't the only one. At least half the girls in their homeroom that day were wearing Rachel Harkness originals. Lately, Rachel had been so busy taking design requests that she rarely had time to daydream about an escape to New York. When she *did* fantasize about her future fashion shows, she pictured models with bodies of all shapes and sizes, like those of her friends.

She knew she'd get to that career someday. But she no longer minded the fact that someday was years way. For now, she was content in Slayton, where there still wasn't much to do, but she had plenty of pals to do not much with.

Where there was a boy who somehow seemed to get sweeter and cuter with each day Rachel knew him.

And where a girl named Lily had become a lifelong friend, even if (technically) she wasn't quite alive.

POISON APPLE BOOKS

The Dead End

This Totally Bites!

Miss Fortune

Now You See Me...

Midnight Howl

Her Evil Twin

Curiosity Killed the Cat

At First Bite

THRILLING.

BONE-CHILLING.

THESE BOOKS

HAVE BITE!

ROTTEN APPLE BOOKS

READ THEM ALL!

Mean Ghouls

Zombie Dog

Drop-Dead Gorgeous

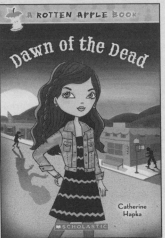

Dawn of the Dead

UNEXPECTED. UNFORGETTABLE.
UNDEAD. GET BITTEN!